BY

JEFF HUTCHEON

WITH T. L. HEYER

Represented by:

WordServe Literary Group, Ltd.

Contact: Greg Johnson
7061 S. University Blvd., Suite 307

Centennial, CO 80122

303.471-6675 (office)

719-232-9603 (cell)

greg@wordserveliterary.com

Published by Authors Place Press
9885 Wyecliff Drive, Suite 200
Highlands Ranch, CO 80126
AuthorsPlace.com

Manufactured in the United States of America.

ISBN: 978-1-62865-739-5

DEDICATED TO:

Sherri, Lindsey, and Peter

Based on a True Story. My story. Our story.

This story is inspired by the author's encounters and experiences with the orphan's spirit through the journey of adoption.

However, *Adopted* is a work of fiction. Names, characters, scenes, and locations are the product of the author's imagination.

Any resemblance to actual events or persons, living or dead, is coincidental.

CONTENTS

PART I

Caroline, age 11

Joseph, age 6

CHAPTER 1

Strapp held his wife's hand as he drove, stealing glances at the photograph she held. This was the only picture they had of their son, a photo they received from their social worker. The boy looked to be about six years old, and he had dark skin, darker eyes, and black hair. Strapp and Julie had never met him, but they knew he was theirs.

"How are you feeling, babe?" Strapp asked as they pulled into the parking lot of the adoption agency.

"I just want to meet him. I know this face so well," Julie said. Her voice sounded nervous and excited as she looked down again into those dark eyes. "I want to know the rest of him."

Julie had printed several copies of his photo, and now they each had one. Strapp carried the photo in his wallet. Caroline, delighted to get a little brother, taped the photo to the inside of her locker at school. And Julie almost always had it in her hand.

His name was Joseph. They had nicknamed him Little Joe.

Finally, this day had come. They were on their way to the agency, taking the next step toward bringing him home. Today, they would learn his story.

Strapp parked the car and turned off the ignition. He turned to his wife: "You're the best mom I know."

Her smile only halfway filled her face. "I hope we can do this. I keep thinking of the horror stories they told us in the foster-parenting classes; all those words about attachment disorders and kids who don't know how to love or be loved."

"Julie, they just say those things to prepare people for the worst, and they probably get some people who have no idea what they're signing up for. People who've never parented at all. I mean, I don't mean to brag… but if they met Caroline, they'd see that we know what we're doing."

Julie smiled. "She is pretty amazing, that girl of ours."

He took her chin in his hand. "And we raised her. You and me. We are good parents. We can do this again. No matter what. We've got this."

She took that familiar deep breath, and he recognized the sound: the moment just before the point of no return.

Strapp squeezed her hand. "You ready?"

She squeezed back, her eyes shining with tears. "I'm ready. Let's go meet our son."

CHAPTER 2

As a seasoned caseworker for more than a decade, Joan Davis had processed more foster placements than she could count, or maybe even remember. At this point in her career, she wasn't interested in counting anymore. Joan no longer allowed time for sentimentality when files were piling high with the names and stories of high maintenance children and even higher maintenance parents. She had this process down to a science of efficiency, and she fully intended to close this file before lunchtime.

Joan had emailed and phoned with Strapp and Julie for weeks now, so it will be good to finally connect faces with their names. She heard two knocks on her office door, and there they were, meeting in person for the first time.

Lord, he's tall, Joan thought.

She stood to greet them, reaching across her desk to shake their hands. "Well, well! Good morning to you, the new parents!"

"Ms. Davis, I'm so glad to meet you, finally," Julie said.

"The pleasure is mine. Please, call me Joan." Julie took Joan's hand into both of hers.

“I believe you have a child who belongs to us?” Strapp said with a smile as she shook his hand as well. His giant palm dwarfed Joan’s.

“Yes, sir, I believe I might! Let’s get started, shall we? I have a lot to tell you.”

They each sat down across from her desk, and Joan opened the folder that held Joseph’s file. She took out a handful of photos, and she lined them up on the desk like scenes from a comic strip. Joan pointed to the first photo on the left.

“Well, here he is. Meet Little Joe. This is the first photo we have of him on the day he came into the system. He was about eighteen months old when this picture was taken. The police gave us this photo. Actually, the police gave us most of these.”

In that first snapshot, Joe was sitting in a large chair next to a metal desk in a police station. He was wearing a t-shirt and a diaper, his hands resting on the green vinyl seat of the chair. He didn’t have a blanket or a teddy bear; he didn’t even have a pair of pants. As toddlers tend to position themselves in chairs too big for them, Little Joe’s legs were splayed straight in front of him, so the dirty soles of his feet faced the camera. His dark eyes looked empty.

Julie picked up the photo, holding it so that both she and Strapp could study it.

Joan read from the file, rattling off details and facts with the level of emotion one might assign to a list of phone numbers.

“Let’s see. Bio mom was a severe drug addict, and Joseph was born addicted to drugs and alcohol from the pregnancy. Bio dad was never determined. Mom would leave on drug binges for days at a time, and there was no adult to step in when mom left him in the house all alone. As you can see here," she offered them the second photo, "the home was in deplorable conditions."

The house was piled high like an episode of *Hoarders.* A tattered couch, a stained coffee table, but nothing of consequence or permanence or…a home. Just piles of newspapers and trash.

In the bottom right corner of the photo, Strapp noticed a small bowl, half-filled with food. "Looks like they had a dog?"

Joan scanned her document with her finger and frowned. "Says here, no pets. No, that was Joseph's bowl. Bio mom would put a can of beans on the floor for him to eat while she was gone."

Julie put her hand to her mouth, stifling a small gasp. Strapp furrowed his brow.

"What's all that? Drug paraphernalia, I assume?" Strapp asked, pointing to the needles and syringes scattered on a coffee table.

"Yes, sir. All within arm's reach of a toddler. That's a no-go for us, as you can imagine."

They sat silently for a minute or so. This was so much to take in for an adult, and yet it had been all this little boy had ever known.

"How did you find him? How did you know this was happening?" Julie asked.

Joan looked up from the file. "Sad story. Bio Mom had a court hearing for drug charges, and when she went through security at the courthouse, they found drug paraphernalia on her person."

"Right there in the courthouse?" Strapp asked.

"She brought it with her, if you can imagine that. She didn't get her hearing that day, but she got a ride in the cop car over to the station instead. She mentioned a kid, and when the officers went to her address to check, they found Joseph."

"Was he all alone?"

"Not that time. Says here in the file that she had left him with somebody she'd met that morning at the 7-Eleven."

Julie gasped again, finding it harder and harder to breathe as she considered what this small child's life had been. *How could a mother…?*

Joan glanced up at her over the rim of her glasses, took them off, and placed them on her desk. "Mrs. Strapson, with all due respect, I must encourage you to get a handle on your emotions. We have a lot of information to get through here. Unfortunately, if you let it all get to you, we'll never get down the list."

Julie took Strapp's hand. She sat up taller.

"I apologize. I just…"

"I know it's a lot. Believe me, I know."

"How do you hold it all?" Julie whispered.

Joan held Julie's eye contact, dealing with the reality of her emotions that she always tried to keep tucked safely away, separate from her work. "Ma'am, I cannot hold it all. So, I send them on to parents who can."

She opened the file, and she continued with Joseph's story.

"Joseph went into the system when he was just under two years old. A family took him in with the intent to adopt him, but it took about two years for him to become legally free for adoption." She pointed to the next photo in the lineup. A young couple with two blond children, and Joseph.

"One month before the adoption would be finalized, the adoptive mother died from... let's see..." Joan scanned her finger down the page again, looking for a diagnosis or cause of death. "Ah, yes. Here it is. Cancer."

Julie and Strapp looked at the photo. The lovely blonde woman, with the kind and loving face, had died.

Joan prattled on: "Adoptive father decided to go through with the adoption after his wife died, and within three months, he had married his wife's best friend."

She looked up at them over the top of her glasses, "Deduce from *that* what you will."

Strapp raised his eyebrows. Julie swallowed hard.

"So, the dead wife's best friend stepped in as Joseph's third mother figure, and after six months, she had had enough. Something like an ultimatum, I suppose. 'Get rid of the boy, or I'm leaving.'"

"She wanted him to get rid of Joseph?"

"Her agenda for her new family did not include him, it appears."

"So, then what?"

"Well, the adoptive father put Joseph back into the system. Joseph went to live with what we call 'professional foster parents' at that point. They have six foster children living in their home."

"*Six*?" Strapp asked.

"It adds up to federal stipends as income, sir. It's how some people take a paycheck. It sounds like a lot, for sure. Some foster parents truly care for the children they take in. But not all."

"And he's with them now?"

"He is, and I will tell you, this is not a good situation."

"Not… how?"

"There have been some allegations of abuse, and perhaps some, shall we say, *unconventional discipline.* But those are unsubstantiated."

"Please, Ms. Davis—I mean, Joan," Julie said, "How soon can we start the transition into our family?"

Joan closed the file and looked at them. "Well, that's what I wanted to talk to you about today." She took off her glasses, set them on her desk, and folded her hands on top of the closed folder.

"Normally, we would introduce you to everyone on Joseph's care team to begin a transitional phase. That varies among families and placements, but typical progression begins with simply a lunch date with the child. Then you spend a couple of hours together next time, then an overnight visit, and then you'll bring him into your home as foster parents."

"Yes, that's what we learned in our classes," Strapp said.

"That's what we are anticipating," Julie nodded.

"It's actually not what we recommend for Joseph," Joan said.

The air stood still in the room.

"I'd like to recommend that you take him home with you today."

Julie's eyes grew wide.

Strapp said, "What? *Today?*"

"Yes, Mr. Strapson. The care team has discussed Joseph's needs at length. As we consider all the transitions he has experienced, we deem it best for Joseph to have a clean break."

"But...but we...please, we are not prepared to take him home today."

Joan's brow furrowed. "You are not *prepared*?"

Julie thought immediately of their empty guest room. "We have a bedroom for him, and there's a bed. But that is all. I wanted to prepare more of a space to show him we were ready for him."

"Mrs. Strapson, a bed is all he needs. That is more than he has had in his past."

Julie and Strapp looked at each other, wordlessly.

Joan interrupted. "This child has had four mothers, and he is not yet in kindergarten. If you are confident that this is the direction you're headed, and if you intend to make him yours eventually, then we recommend beginning as soon as possible. Permanence is what he needs the most."

Julie and Strapp held each other's gaze. He raised his eyebrows and took a deep breath. She nodded almost imperceptibly.

She watched her husband turn back to face the caseworker, his chin jutted forward, his jaw resolute. Strapp spoke with confidence: "Then today is the day. Let's bring him home."

CHAPTER 3

Strapp had wanted to adopt for a long time, but Julie had not been on board for the last decade or so. Their daughter Caroline was in middle school, a compliant firstborn who lit up their lives, their only child, now eleven years old. Sure, they wanted more children, but some complications with Caroline's birth made it impossible for Julie to be pregnant again. Adoption was their only option for expanding their family, and it was a daunting path. Julie just wasn't sure she could love another child as much as she loved Caroline.

Hers was a valid fear, one that Strapp had to admit that he felt too. So, he had let the topic rest for an entire decade. He had learned long ago not to push his will into their marriage. A win for him wasn't a win for them, and he wouldn't grow their family by sheer force of his own agenda. So, he waited, and he loved Caroline for all he was worth, fully aware that she might be his one and only chance at fatherhood.

But everything had changed one Sunday when their pastor shared his family's story of adopting two boys from Africa. Strapp looked over to see Julie crying uncontrollably. I mean, it wasn't that unusual; she's a crier, especially in church. But, boy, she was *crying.* Mascara, tissues, the whole deal.

When they got into the car after church, Strapp asked gently, "So, what was that about? What's on your mind this morning?"

She took a deep breath like she was gathering her courage to jump off a cliff. "We're supposed to adopt."

Strapp still remembers the rush of emotion, how his face broke into a smile. "Really?"

"Yes. I'm sure of it. The Lord showed me his face."

"Whose face?"

"Our son. He showed me the face of our son, honey. I know what he looks like, and we have to find him."

She described for her husband the dark skin and eyes, the black hair, how he looked like he might be Hispanic or Latino. She said, "I don't know his name, but I know his face. We need to find him, Strapp. He's our son."

And the ball started rolling. They soon took classes to become licensed foster parents, and they registered with an agency that cared for the highest percentage of his demographic, as best as they could tell. They began working with a caseworker, and Julie waited anxiously to see a picture of the face that matched the one in her vision. They waited and waded through the photos of many, many—so very many—children. An overwhelming number of young faces longing for families to call their own. But Julie was certain: she would know him when she saw him.

On the day Joan had emailed them this photo, they met their son on the screen. Julie had cried when she saw him, as if she were meeting someone again—and yet for the very first time.

"That's him."

• • •

For so long, the wallet-sized photo was all they had, so it felt surreal to hear Joan set the plan in motion. With the nod from Julie and the word from Strapp, Joan called Joseph's foster mom to tell her to gather his things, and they agreed to meet at the park at 1:00 pm. Like a starter pistol launches a race, everything started to move. Sure enough, Joan closed her file before lunchtime.

They had about two hours to grab lunch and prepare a place for their new son, so Julie got on the phone with her girlfriends. Like a practiced pit crew, her friends raced to her house and pulled off a dozen details. They transformed the guest bedroom into a little boy's den: blue sheets, red pillows, and a fluffy comforter; a bookshelf stocked with picture books; a cityscape rug with a map of streets for matchbox cars. They put his name on the wall in wooden block letters, and they tied red and blue helium balloons to the banister in the foyer.

Strapp and Julie had one last stop to make before they went to the park: Caroline's school. The school secretary summoned her to the main office, and Caroline arrived a few minutes later with her backpack and some questions. "Do I have an orthodontist appointment or something? Why are you both here?"

"Honey, we have some news," Julie said, taking Caroline's hand.

Caroline looked back and forth between her parents. "You guys are acting weird. I'm kind of freaking out right now."

Strapp and Julie glanced at one another, smiling. He said, "Yeah, we are, too."

"Caroline, how would you like to meet Joe today?"

Her face lit up, and she clapped her hands. "Joe? Today?!"

"Today, sweetheart," Julie said.

"Yes, please!" She swung open the door to the office, just as the bell rang for students to switch classes. The hallway buzzed with students, conversations, and lockers opening and closing. "Stay close, you guys," Caroline grinned. "It gets crazy here. Don't worry, though, I'm a trained professional."

Caroline winked at them and entered the loud mass of middle schoolers. They followed her long blonde hair and backpack as she navigated the foot traffic to forge a path out the front door.

"Look how happy she is," Julie said, adoringly.

"She's been waiting for this day, too." Strapp held the door open for Julie.

Caroline was already halfway to the car.

• • •

Little Joe was at the top of the sliding board when they spotted him for the first time. They watched from inside the car as he soared down the slide, his bottom landing with a thud in the woodchips. He hopped up and ran back to the ladder to do it all again.

Several children played near him, but not with him.

"Those must be the other children he lives with," Strapp said.

"*Lived* with," Caroline corrected her dad. She had leaned forward into the front seat, her head between her parents. She linked her hands in each of their elbows. "He is going to live with *us* now."

"Hello, Joseph," Julie whispered.

"We've been waiting for you, buddy," Strapp said quietly.

"And I'm your sister," Caroline whispered. Her hands cupped her mouth like a megaphone, like she was whispering a loud secret.

They waited another moment before they got out of the car. It felt so bizarre watching the little boy play. Not often can one be so aware of a seismic shift; of the moments before everything changes forever.

Strapp held out his hand toward his wife and daughter. His palm was an open invitation for their family handshake, a tradition they started before Caroline's first day of preschool. Julie placed her hand on his. Caroline placed hers on top, with her palm face down. Long ago, Caroline had named it a "Hand Sandwich."

"Family first," Strapp said.

"And family last," Julie added.

"And family always," Caroline finished.

• • •

There was one adult in the park, a woman seated on a park bench. She had an infant in her arms, an empty stroller nearby, and a cardboard box beside her.

"You must be Joe's family," she said, standing to greet them. She immediately began the telltale mom bounce that all moms do when they're soothing a fussy baby. Julie remembered it well. Every mom does it, even foster moms.

"My name is Becca. My husband and I are the—oh, one second, I'm sorry—*Nicholas*!" She interrupted herself, shouting to one of the children. "Nicholas! You don't push her off that swing. Do you understand me? I said *no pushing*." Just as casually, she turned her attention back to Strapp, Julie, and Caroline. "Sorry. Never a dull moment. My husband and I are the foster parents of this whole crew."

She was bouncing and patting the baby as Strapp held out his hand to introduce himself. She rebuffed his offer. "Sorry. Hands full. It's nice to—*Nicholas!*—nice to meet you."

She turned to the bench and gestured to the box. "That's Joe's stuff, and he's good to go. He's already had lunch, so..." Bounce, bounce.

Julie took a step closer to Becca. "I'd like to thank you for all you've done for Joseph."

"Sure." Bounce, bounce. She made quick eye contact with Julie. "You're welcome. Thanks for taking him off my hands."

"Yes, sure, of course." Julie didn't know what to say. She didn't know the script for this kind of changing of the guard.

"Should we go talk to him?" Strapp asked. "Or, will you introduce us? How does this work?"

"I'll stay here. It's best for me to keep as many eyes on everybody as I can. You can take it from here, and I'll make sure the others give you some space while you all get acquainted. I think he's in the sandbox."

They didn't want to overwhelm Joe, so they had decided in advance that Julie would be the first one to approach him. Julie walked over to the sandbox and sat down next to Joe. With his fist firmly wrapped around a little red plastic shovel, he was piling sand into a toy dump truck. She sat down beside him, quietly.

"Hello, there, Joseph."

Joe glanced at her for a moment, then he went back to shoveling sand.

"My name is Julie."

He shoveled sand. He didn't look up. He didn't speak.

"Can I build with you?"

She slipped out of her sandals and put her feet in the sand. The sandbox was scattered with trucks, shovels, and pails. She turned a pail onto its side and began scooping sand into it.

"Are you the mom?"

The mom. Like she was *any* mom. As far as he knew, she was just another mom, a fictional mom in a make-believe family.

Oh, sweet boy, she thought. Out loud, she said, "I am. But you can call me Julie, if you'd like."

He was quiet. All his attention belonged to the shovel and the truck. Julie looked over to Strapp and Caroline waiting and watching in the distance. They were waiting for her to give the wave or the beckon or the thumbs up, anything to show them it was time. But it wasn't quite time.

"Can I show you something cool?" Julie asked. "Check this out, Joseph."

She filled the pail with sand, packing it with her fist and smoothing it across the top.

"The bucket looks like it's full, right? But watch this trick. It's like magic."

She carried the pail to the drinking fountain next to the sandbox and pressed the button, letting the water pour into the pail, saturating the sand.

"We thought it was full but look. There's room for some more." She pressed the sand with her fingertips, packing it in. She carried the full bucket back to the sandbox, placing it upside down in the sand pile.

She whispered, "This is my favorite part. Can you help me?"

Joe's hands were still. He paused his shoveling, and he glanced sideways at the bucket.

Julie knocked on the sides of the upside-down bucket. "Knock, knock."

Joe watched.

She knocked again. "Knock, knock. Knock, knock. You want to try?"

She looked to Joe. He stared at the bucket.

"Knock, knock," she tapped, once more on each side. She lifted the pail, sliding it off to reveal the perfect mold of sand, complete with the scalloped design from the inside of the pail.

Joe's eyes widened. It was hard to imagine that no one had ever taught him to build a sandcastle, but the miracle was brand new to him.

"Again," he said.

"Again? Okay, let's do it again."

She repeated the steps, piling the sand into the pail, smoothing it across the top, then filling it with water. This time, when she knocked on the pail, Joe reached over to knock, too.

"Knock, knock," she said.

"Knock, knock," he repeated after her.

She lifted the pail to make the second pillar of their castle.

This time, Joe smiled.

"Again," he said.

"Again!" she said. As Julie piled sand into the pail once more, she looked up to Strapp and Caroline. She nodded, and they walked toward the sandbox.

"I have some helpers to build our castle with us," she said. "See them? This is our family. Can they build, too?"

Strapp squatted next to the sandbox, making himself just a little less tall. Caroline slipped off her shoes and put her toes in the sand.

"Hi, buddy," Strapp said, reaching for a pail.

Joe piled sand into the pail. Caroline used a shovel to help him fill it up.

Using Joe's word choices, Julie said, "Let's have the dad put the water in this time."

She handed the pail to Strapp, and he filled it with water. When he came back, he slipped off his shoes and sat down with them on the edge of the sandbox. He turned it upside down in the sand.

"Ready, Joe? Show them how you do it."

Only Joe's eyes moved. He glanced at Julie, then Strapp, then Caroline.

"Knock, knock," he said, tapping his little fist on the side.

They each took a turn.

"Knock, knock."

"Knock, knock."

"Knock, knock."

This time, Strapp lifted the pail—a third pillar in their castle.

Joe made direct eye contact with Strapp and said, "Again."

"You bet, pal," Strapp said. "Let's do it, again."

Together they built their sandcastle, complete with four pillars, a tree branch flagpole, and a respectable moat around the perimeter. Every good castle needs a moat.

"Hey, Joe," Strapp asked, as he sand sculpted an "S" for Strapson, "do you like ice cream?"

Joe nodded.

"Sweet. I was hoping you'd say yes. How about we go get some ice cream together, and then we can show you your new home?"

"Yes, please."

Strapp carried the cardboard box that held everything Joe owned, and Little Joe walked beside him to the car. Just a few strides behind, Caroline and Julie followed; Caroline whispered, "Did you hear that, Mom? He already says *please.*"

They left the park and the foster family behind, and they took Joe to get some ice cream. When in doubt, a scoop of ice cream is always a great start to a new life together.

CHAPTER 4

After months of dreaming, planning, praying, and feeling like time was slowing to a crawl, suddenly in the dizzying whirlwind of one morning and afternoon, Joe was here to stay. Strapp and Julie created routines and structure and a sense of belonging. They showed him his own toothbrush in the bathroom, and his very own seat at the dinner table. They had pancakes in the mornings, and they read bedtime stories at night. They helped him begin to understand "home" as a place, an idea, and a feeling.

Julie took him shopping for new clothes, new shoes, and a new backpack for school. Strapp taught Joe how to dribble a basketball in the driveway, and he lifted him high to dunk the ball in the hoop. Caroline taught him the basic essentials for being a kid in their family. She taught him how to play *Sorry!* She explained, "I know it's weird that you have to draw a One or a Two to take your guy out of the Start Circle, but the Two is especially great because you get to draw again." She showed him how to set the table: "See, it's like a family," she taught him. "The plate is the mom, so she's in the middle. The knife is the dad, so he stands beside her on this side. The spoon is the sister—that's me—and the fork is the brother. That's you, Joe." And she taught him how to make the Hand Sandwich. She showed him how to place his hand on hers, and she taught him the words one phrase at a time: "Family first, family last, family always."

As they introduced Joe to his new life as a Strapson, they found glimpses of how much he had done without. Some of his discoveries were endearing, like when he called their home "the hotel" since a four-bedroom house was the largest he had ever known. For days after they showed him to his new bedroom, he still stored all his items in his cardboard box from the foster home. He didn't understand that he could make the space his own. The clothes in the closet were *his* to wear. The books on the shelves were *his* to enjoy. He didn't know what to do with a promise of permanence. As he learned how much they wanted to give him, they became painfully aware of how little he had in the past.

He became part of their family in the same way that one falls in love: a little at a time, and then somehow, all at once. Little Joe soaked up this new life and all of this love like a thirsty sponge, like this was what he had been waiting for his whole life, and in many ways, it was.

• • •

Suddenly, the family photo collages on the wall felt woefully incomplete. After all, those photos showed a family of three, and they were now a family of *four.* Julie made an appointment for a family photo session by the lake—another first for Little Joe, and he was delighted by the sheer volume of so much sand. Splashing, piggyback rides, more sandcastles, and so much laughter filled the day. The photographer captured the essence of who they had become. Julie ordered prints upon prints, and she filled every frame in their home.

A family of four is an even number, a perfect square. Everybody had somebody.

• • •

Mealtimes were important in the Strapson home as they all gathered together at the table. They prayed together, asking God to bless their meal, and they talked about their day. They discussed what had happened, the good and the bad, and they listened to each other. The dinner table was their connecting place.

One evening, as everyone took their places at the table, pulling out their chairs and putting napkins in their laps, Joe said, "Could I pray for our dinner tonight?"

Somehow, it hadn't crossed their minds yet that he would want to, that he might know how to talk to God. But yes—yes, of course, he could be the one to pray over their dinner.

"I'd love that, Joseph. Thank you," Strapp said, bowing his head.

"Dear God, I thank you for my new family, for my mom, and my dad, and my sister. Thank you for food. Amen."

"Amen," they each repeated after him.

"Thank you, Joe," Strapp said, reaching for the plate of roast beef.

Joe's words were so pure and true, and he prayed what was on his mind. He prayed like he was talking to somebody he knew.

• • •

At bedtime one night, Joe climbed onto the couch next to Julie, ready for her to read his bedtime story.

"Hey, pal," Julie said, as he snuggled in beside her. "Which book would you like to hear tonight?"

"This one," he said, as he held up the children's book of Bible stories. It had been on the shelf in his bedroom, and he pulled it down for the first time.

"Oh, that's one of my favorites, Joseph! What a great choice. I love stories from the Bible."

"Me, too," Joe said. "Can you read the one about the whale? I like that one."

Julie looked at him, surprised. "You know the one about the whale?"

"Yes. I like that one."

"Well, you bet. Let's read that one."

She opened to the story of Jonah, and she read to Little Joe about the man who spent three days in the belly of a big fish because he had disobeyed God. Joseph giggled when the fish threw up, when Jonah landed on dry land, all covered in whale goo.

"That's my favorite part," he said.

As an experiment to see what he knew, she said, "Joe, what other stories do you like in this book?"

Joe started at the beginning, and he began flipping through the pages, telling parts of each story. He told about the snake in the tree with the apple, and he talked about the animals on Noah's boat. He told her about David and the giant, about Daniel and the lions, and he pointed out Joseph's coat. He showed her a picture of Jesus on the cross, and he said, "Jesus died. And he came back."

"He sure did, buddy. He sure did."

Someone has read the Bible to this child, Julie thought.

"Hey, Joe? Can you tell me who made you?"

"God made me," he said.

"You're right, sweetheart. God made you. And he loves you."

"And I love God," Joe said, turning another page.

Julie felt goose bumps on her arms, and her eyes filled with tears. She kissed the top of her son's head.

Sometimes, Joe surprised them with the most invaluable things he already knew.

CHAPTER 5

On the morning of Joe's seventh birthday, Strapp and Julie woke Caroline early to decorate the breakfast table with balloons, streamers, and a banner. When Joe came to the table, bleary-eyed and half awake, his eyes grew suddenly wide at the sight of a birthday cupcake on his plate.

"Happy Birthday to you!" his family sang to him as Julie put a birthday crown on his head.

"Happy Birthday," Joe had said over and over again, as if the phrase was new to him. He seemed to think it was something you say in return; like when someone says, "thank you," and the appropriate reply is "you're welcome." Each time they said, "Happy Birthday," he said it right back to them.

For the last six years, Joe's birthday had merely been a fact on the calendar. It had been rarely acknowledged, and it had certainly never been celebrated. All of that was about to change because birthdays are a big deal in the Strapson family.

Julie baked a three-tiered chocolate cake, and Joe declared it the biggest cake he had ever seen.

They gave him a shiny red bike, and Joe cheered, "That's the coolest bike in the whole wide world! Look at those fat tires—I could climb anything with that bike!"

They gave him a new basketball, and he dribbled it across the kitchen.

They gave him a basketball jersey, and he put it on right away.

Strapp said, "Hey, pal, since you're seven now, I wonder… would you like to play on a basketball team?"

Joe's eyes grew wide. "A *real* team? Really?"

"A real team. And if you want, I could be your coach."

"You know how to be a *basketball coach?*"

"I sure do, buddy! I'd love to be yours."

"A coach!" Joe said, leaping into Strapp's arms.

It was the first time Joe had initiated a hug with anyone in his new family, and Strapp wrapped his arms around his boy, hugging him right back.

That night Joe added a new step to the bedtime routine: a bedtime hug for each of them.

On his seventh birthday, Joe wasn't the only one receiving a gift he had long wanted.

• • •

Strapp volunteered to coach the youngest basketball team in the league, the Vipers. They had ten boys on their team, all six and seven years old, and Joe fit right in. Nobody was very good, which is to be expected with a team of first grade boys. Everybody was new learning what to do with their hands, their feet, and this big orange ball.

At their Saturday morning practices, Strapp taught them the beginning skills of how to handle the ball, pass to teammates, and shoot. For a long time, that mostly resulted in the young boys chasing the wayward ball across the gym, but they were learning. Strapp could often hear the memory of his dad's coaching voice in his head, "Keep at it, son. We all start somewhere."

On the day of their first game, Joe was up earliest, ready to go. Hours before the game, he came into Strapp and Julie's bedroom dressed in his red jersey and holding the ball under his arm. "Dad, you should get in the shower. We have a big day. I need a healthy breakfast, Mom. Dad does, too. Athletes have to be strong."

Strapp opened his eyes and Julie stretched herself awake. "Let's do it, bud."

"Cheerios, please!"

"Cheerios it is," she said, putting on her robe.

"Dad? Are you up?"

"I'm getting up, pal," Strapp said. "It's game day."

"Can I be the starter, Dad? Can I jump first?"

"Let's get some breakfast, pal."

• • •

The gym is a busy place on game day. It was bustling with teams, families, cheering, the whistles of officials, and the squeak of sneakers on the gym floor. Caroline and Julie were dressed in red as they sat in the front row of the bleachers, cheering for the boys by name.

Strapp pulled his team together to warm up, and they ran a few drills on the court, just as they had in practices. He had even taught them a couple of plays, and they impressed him by remembering where to be. What they lacked in ability, they made up for in enthusiasm. These boys were ready to play.

The teams took their places on the court, just as Strapp had taught them. Joe came to the center court for the jump ball.

"Know who you're guarding, boys!" Strapp called from the sideline. "Which basket are we shooting at?"

They pointed down the court to their basket.

"You got it, guys! Let's go!"

The official tossed the ball into the air, Joe's opponent jumped quick, and he tipped the ball over Joe's head. The ball was in play, and the Vipers sprung into defensive action.

Except for Joe. He didn't move.

The Vipers traveled down the court, following the ball, watching for their chance to show off their skills. Joe stayed at center court. Frozen.

"Joe! Let's go!" Strapp called out. "Joe! Where's the ball, buddy? Let's get in the game, pal!"

Joe didn't move. He didn't even blink. He was frozen in place.

Something had happened, something within him had been triggered.

The referee blew the whistle, Strapp ran out to his son.

"Hey, pal, you've got this. You okay?"

Joe said nothing. He looked at Strapp with a blank face.

"It's all right, buddy. Let's take a break."

With his arm around Joe's shoulders, Strapp walked Joe to the bench to have a seat. He put another boy in the game. He knelt in front of Joe. "It's okay, bud. It's okay."

Joe didn't seem disappointed or embarrassed. He seemed like he was in shock.

Julie moved over to sit behind Joe. She put her hand on his back. "Hey, pal, you okay?"

"I'm okay," he said, finally.

"You did great out there," she said, wondering what had happened.

He knew what to do when he and Strapp played together at home, and he could hold his own even in practices. But in a full gym, with sounds and sights and busyness, he froze. It was their first indication of some trauma in Joe's mind, of what happens when Joe is overstimulated. Something in him zoned out.

For the rest of the season, Joe attended all the practices, and he played ball every night with Strapp. On game days, he kept his team hydrated with water bottles at the ready. He came to every game, and he cheered from the sidelines. That's where he wanted to be.

CHAPTER 6

"Mr. Strapson, please introduce your family," the judge said.

The courtroom was smaller than Strapp had expected, nothing like what he had seen on television. But this was family probate court, not criminal court, and everything felt more intimate here.

Strapp and Julie had been sworn in, each of them raising their right hand, promising to tell the truth. The hearing was not public, but the Strapsons had been welcomed to invite their chosen witnesses. The courtroom was packed with people who loved them—grandparents, aunts, uncles, a couple of cousins, and Julie's friends, the women who had prepared their home for Joseph when everything had come together so quickly. Joan, their social worker, sat in the second row right behind the Strapsons. Most endearingly, Joseph's teacher had brought the entire first grade class on a field trip to witness his adoption. His classmates sat straight and tall, filling every seat in the jury box.

Strapp's chair squeaked against the floor as he rose again before the judge.

"Yes, Your Honor. My name is Henry Strapson, Jr., and this is my wife Julie. We've been married for seventeen years, and this is our daughter Caroline." Caroline straightened her skirt and folded her hands in her lap.

Strapp paused, unsure if he could call Joe his son before the judge made it official. "And this is Joseph."

Strapp felt tears prickling his eyes as he looked at this boy he loved so much. Joe sat on his hands, and his feet swung underneath his chair. Strapp cleared his throat, swallowed, and looked back to the judge.

"You have a beautiful family, Mr. Strapson," the judge said, looking down the line of the family.

"Yes, Your Honor. I do."

"I have spoken with your social worker, I have listened to your retained attorney, and now I'd like to hear from you. Tell me, what are your intentions in this courtroom today?"

Strapp reached for Julie's hand. She rose to stand beside him. "Your Honor, my wife and I would like to petition you to grant the adoption of this young man as our son."

"I see. I have reviewed the dates on your paperwork, and I understand this process has happened faster than most."

"Yes, Your Honor," Strapp said. "Joseph has lived in many places, and upon the advice of the care team, we wanted to give him his forever home as soon as possible."

"And do you understand that this is a permanent commitment, even in the event of an ended marriage, death, or other tragic occurrence?"

"Yes, Your Honor," Strapp said.

"Mrs. Strapson, do you agree that this adoption should take place?"

Julie's voice was confident and firm. "Yes, Your Honor."

"And do each of you agree to provide this young man with a loving home?"

They nodded. "Yes, Your Honor."

"And do you understand that with the granting of this request, you will become parents of this child in all respects, just as if he had been born to you?"

"Yes, Your Honor."

"And do you understand that you will be undertaking the intellectual, spiritual, and moral guidance of Joseph?"

"Yes, Your Honor."

"Do you understand that he will become your legal heir?"

"Yes, Your Honor."

"Do you understand that you will be called upon to provide love, affection, encouragement, and that this may not always be convenient?"

"Yes, Your Honor."

"Joseph, what do you call these people?"

Joe looked up at Strapp. "Mom and Dad."

The judge looked to Caroline. "And would you like to become a sister?"

Caroline blushed. "Yes, please—I mean—yes, Your Honor. Please."

There was a certain charm attached to the judge addressing her.

"You are willing to share your parents' attention, affection, and resources?"

"Yes, Your Honor."

"And do you agree that you have room for him in your home?"

"Yes, Your Honor."

"And in your heart?"

"Yes, Your Honor."

"I see. Then let's make this official."

He picked up his pen and signed the decree before him, then he neatly stacked the pages into a pile. He looked out at their family. "Now, before I make a final declaration, we have one more detail to address."

Strapp held his breath. Julie squeezed his hand. They had not expected any further questions… had something come up?

He opened a black box on the bench. He pulled out a gavel, tied with a satin blue ribbon. "By the power vested in me, I have the authority to use any gavel I choose."

The judge looked up at the family, smiling for the first time.

"Based on the testimony of all those involved, this court finds the granting of your petition to be in the best interests of Joseph."

The judge raised the gavel and it hovered as his words rang in the air.

"Mr. and Mrs. Strapson, Caroline and Joseph, it is official and hereby ordered. Today, you are a *family*."

He dropped his gavel with a bang, and the sound seemed to echo in Strapp's chest. It felt like a door closing. A commitment made. A calm assurance. *He is my son.*

The courtroom erupted with the applause of their friends and family. The first graders cheered and clapped their hands.

The Strapson family stood to their feet as the judge came from behind his bench. He held the gavel out to Joseph. "Young man, this is for you."

Joseph held the gavel in his hand. Strapp peered over Joe's shoulder to see the gift. There was a gold plaque on the handle, inscribed with the words: "Joseph Strapson. Son."

"A photo, shall we?" the judge said. He extended his arm, a gesture to invite them to stand beside him. Strapp, Julie, and Caroline huddled around Joe, and the room sparkled with flashes of iPhones and cameras.

"Joseph, hold your gavel high, young man," the judge said. "This is your day."

PART II

A few months later

Caroline, age 12

Joseph, age 7

CHAPTER 7

The Strapson family had settled into what is known far and wide as "the honeymoon phase." In foster parenting classes, the experts warn you about this phase. They tell you how good it will feel, how sweet it all becomes, and how easy it is to think everything will just keep rolling smoothly. They tell you it's fleeting, and they tell you to prepare for the end of the honeymoon. They do not mention a sad reality: nothing can truly prepare you for the end of the honeymoon.

A few months into their life together, it all changed one night.

They had finished eating dinner. Caroline was doing her homework at the dining room table, Julie was drying the dishes, and Strapp was sitting on the living room floor with Joe. They had played together with the wooden set of train tracks, and Strapp was helping Joe snap the magnetic train cars together.

"Joe," Strapp said, "let's put these together and drive them around the village, and then we'll take a break tonight. It's almost time for bath and books."

The evening structure was set, and 7:00 was the nightly time for bath and books.

"No," Joe answered, snapping another car into place.

"Yes, sir," Strapp answered. "Do you want to add one more car or two?" He recalled the parenting strategies that worked with Caroline when she was Joe's age. The best parenting books said that when you give children choices, they feel empowered. Anytime you can, give them a choice between one thing and something else. While they're young, they don't yet realize that the choices are still an act of obedience, so everybody wins.

"I'm not done," Joe said.

"You can choose to put on one more car, or two more cars."

Joe crashed the two train cars together. "No."

"Joe, be gentle with the train cars, please, or we cannot play with them."

Joe smashed them together again. A little black wheel fell off one of the cars and clattered across the wood floor.

"Not okay, buddy. I can see you've made your choice. We have to put these away tonight." Strapp took the plastic lid off the Rubbermaid container, and he began to put the wooden train pieces inside.

"I said, *no!*" Joe crashed the train cars together, smashing them like cymbals.

"Joe—" Strapp reached over to pick him up, and he felt a blow to the bridge of his nose. Joe had punched him in the face with the train car.

Strapp reeled back, his hands holding his nose. His fingers looked blurry as he checked to see if he was bleeding. Joe had clocked him—*hard.*

"Strapp? Honey?" Julie rushed into the living room, holding a dish towel. "What happened?!"

Caroline gasped and jumped to her feet, her pencil falling to the floor.

"I'm okay," Strapp held up his hand to stop them from coming closer. He answered Julie's words and Caroline's eyes. "I'm okay. It's okay."

He knelt again to pick up Joe. This time, Joe spit in his face.

"I hate you!" Joe shouted. "You're never going to be my dad!"

Joe launched into a tirade of anger that this family had never seen before. All his fury came out at once. He screamed, shouted, and writhed on the floor. Strapp scooped him up, wrapping his arms around Joe's body to keep the little boy safe from injuring himself. Joe threw his head back in full force, bashing Strapp in the nose once more—this time, with the back of his skull. Strapp's nose began to bleed.

Julie rushed closer to the scene, but she wasn't sure how to help. Those two were engaged in a wrestling match on the floor, blood pouring from Strapp's nose, and Joe thrashing violently like a squirrel caught in a trap.

Joe shouted on repeat, "I hate you! I hate you! *I hate you!*"

Strapp wrapped his arms firmly around Joe, an anchor in the storm. Joe's thrashing turned to wailing, and the wailing faded to crying.

Strapp held him safe until Joe gave up the fight. The little boy's body softened in Strapp's arms.

Joe's episode had lasted for minutes that felt like hours, draining both the father and son in every way. With Joe calm once more, Strapp had handed him over to Julie, and she carried him to bed. The boy went from raging to sleeping in a matter of moments. He had drained himself to the very last drop.

• • •

Strapp stood in the bathroom, holding a warm washcloth to his face and gently washing away the layers of blood, both wet and dry. His t-shirt looked like he had been shot. He stripped off the t-shirt and tossed it into the bathroom trash and looked into the mirror. His eyes were already ringed with dark circles from the blow to his face.

How much worse would this look tomorrow?

He dropped the washcloth into the dirty clothes hamper, and he reached for the bathroom towel. He dried his face, holding the towel still, careful not to bump his nose.

His face hurt.

But his heart was broken.

He leaned over the sink, and then he began to weep into the towel.

Though Joe was fast asleep, Strapp couldn't stop hearing his words.

I hate you.

You're not my dad.

You'll never be my dad.

Strapp cried into the towel, letting the thick cotton muffle the sound of his voice.

Oh, God. That was awful. I don't know what went wrong. I don't know how it happened so fast. I love him so much. He's our boy... he is my son. Why is he rejecting me?

In the silence of the bathroom, Strapp heard an audible reply.

"Now you know how I feel."

He lowered the towel from his face, and he looked around. Nobody was there. He was alone. He looked in the mirror, leaning close. He heard the words again. From inside his spirit.

Now you know how I feel.

• • •

Strapp was laying on his back in their bed when Julie came into their bedroom. From beneath the cool cloth on his face, he heard the bedroom door open and close softly. He felt her take his hand.

"I have some ice for you," she said, her voice tender. "May I?"

He winced as he felt the pressure of the compress across his forehead, his eyes, and the bridge of his nose. Julie gently touched the top of his head, softly combing her fingers through his dark hair.

He reached out for her with his eyes closed. He felt for his wife's hand, letting himself be soothed by her.

"Is he in bed?" he asked.

"Sound asleep," she said.

"Is Caroline okay?"

"She's okay—a little shaken. I think we all are."

Strapp exhaled. "He said he hates me."

"I know, baby. I heard him."

"He said I'm not his dad."

Julie whispered, "I heard that, too."

Strapp was silent. He thought about the voice he'd heard in the bathroom.

Julie spoke into their stillness. "Honey, earlier today, Caroline got out some photo albums. She sat with Joe on the couch and she told him some stories of our family before he came home to us. She was pointing out different people, her cousins, grandparents, your mom and dad… she was naming them all."

"Do you think that's what started this?"

"I don't know what started this, except that they told us this could happen, Strapp. We must remember that. Just like we have a lot of memories before him, he has a lot of history before he came to us. We may never know all that Joe has experienced."

After another beat of silence, she said, "It was good to see those pictures of your dad again, honey."

Strapp felt a heaviness deep in his chest, the weight of sadness and remembering.

"I need him," Strapp whispered.

"I know, sweetheart."

Julie watched as a tear rolled from underneath the compress on Strapp's face. She reached for him, letting the tear roll over the back of her finger before it streamed into the hollow of his ear.

"Honey," she said, "the pictures of your dad brought back so many memories of him. I was thinking about that friend of your dad's. That mentor he loved so much."

"Hank?"

"Hank. Yes. That's the one."

"I haven't talked to him since Dad's funeral."

"I haven't either, but I remember what he said to you that day." She stroked the back of Strapp's palm. "Remember, honey? He said you'd never be alone."

"I remember. Yes."

She waited a moment, and then she said, "Strapp, this may seem strange for me to be talking about it all right now. And I don't know… I can't get him out of my mind. In all my remembering today, one thing led to another… did you know we have the guestbook from your dad's memorial service on the bookshelf?"

He swallowed.

"Hank's name was in there. Most people only wrote their address, but he wrote down his phone number, too."

Strapp lifted the ice pack just enough to peer out at her, to see that Julie held a notecard in her hand.

"I think he could help us, honey," Julie said.

Strapp lowered the ice pack onto his face once more, wincing again.

"Hank is not my dad," Strapp said.

"But he knew your dad. He loved your dad.

Strapp didn't speak. Julie put the card on the bedside table.

"Just an idea, honey. Get some rest."

She rose to stand beside him, and she lifted his hand to her face. As she kissed his hand, she felt the warmth of his wedding ring on her lips.

CHAPTER 8

"I appreciate you meeting with me, Hank," Strapp said. "This probably feels strange to hear from me."

Hank's eyes twinkled when he smiled. He was an old man by most standards, older than Strapp's dad would be. But Hank's mind was sharp and his heart young. His eyes carried the kind of wisdom that comes not only from intellectual knowledge, but from a life well-lived.

"Oh, it's not as strange as you might think," Hank said. "I was hoping I'd hear from you someday. It's the benefit of living in the same house all these years. Same address, same phone number. I was maybe even waiting for your call."

"That's kind of you, sir."

"Your dad was a good friend of mine, Strapp. He was one in a million."

"He sure was."

"You sure do look like him."

Strapp smiled, looking down into his black coffee. "He always said I looked like he spit me out."

Hank's laughter was warm. "Sounds like your Pop. I would agree with that."

Hank waited for Strapp's eyes to meet his again. And then he asked, "How can I help you, son?"

"I need some guidance, sir."

"He and I had a few conversations that started like this one."

Strapp shook his head. "It's hard to imagine my dad needing help."

"We all do, now and then," Hank said. "Tell me about yourself, Strapp. It's been a few years. Give me some headlines."

"Yes, sir," Strapp said, and he began to tell Hank the story of his family. It had been a decade since Strapp's dad had died, a decade since Strapp had spoken with Hank. There were a lot of years and headlines to cover. He told Hank about Julie, then about Caroline, and then about Joe.

"That's my family, Hank. That's my boy, Joseph. We call him Little Joe. Or, just Joe, actually."

Strapp held his phone up to show the captured moment he loved so much, the day the adoption was finalized. They were all standing in front of the judge's bench, huddled in a half-circle around Joe with his gavel high in the air.

Hank pulled his glasses out of his chest pocket. Putting them on, he leaned across the table to get a closer look.

"Well, hello there," Hank said, taking the phone. He touched the screen, enlarging the image. The lines around his eyes wrinkled. "Caroline and Little Joe. I love them already."

"We do, too. It's been so good, Hank."

Hank's eyes looked up to meet Strapp's. He knew Strapp was holding back, and his gaze pressed Strapp for more of the truth. He said, "That shiner on your face looks… exceptional."

"Yeah… Actually, I guess I'd say it's been mostly good," Strapp said.

Hank set the phone down on the table next to his coffee cup. "Tell me what's going on, Strapp."

Strapp leaned back in his chair. He ran his hands through his hair, then folded his arms across his chest. "I don't know what we've gotten ourselves into."

He told Hank about the battle over the toy train, the night when everything changed.

Strapp said, "Hank, I saw everything they had warned us about in the parenting classes—except ten times worse than anything I imagined. He lashed out with the worst possible tirade, shouting the meanest, most hateful things a person could say. He said he hates me."

"Do you think he really hates you? Or do you think he was just angry?"

"I don't know. I mean, he was *definitely* angry. But since then, his whole countenance has changed in our home. It's like we saw a different boy for those first few months. I feel like I've truly met my son for the first time. I'm getting a glimpse of who he really might be, and it appears that my wife and I have adopted a child who does not want to be in our family. I feel like, if he just knew how much we love him, how much we want him to be ours, then he would…"

"Then he would what?"

Strapp's shoulders sank. "Then he would want us too. He would love us in return."

"Strapp, do you think you could ever help him understand how much you love him? Can something like that be quantified?"

Strapp folded his hands.

"Hank, I have to tell you this strange thing that happened. On the night of that fight, I went to the bathroom to clean myself up while Julie was putting Joe to bed. I was all alone, Hank, but I heard a voice. Clear as I can hear yours right now."

"Yeah? What did it say?"

Strapp leaned in to whisper the words. "*Now you know how I feel.*"

Hank put his elbows on the table, and he steepled his fingers together. "*Now you know how I feel,*" Hank repeated. "Well, that is very interesting, indeed."

"Weird, right?"

"I didn't say *weird*. I said *interesting*. What do you think it was?" Hank asked.

Strapp looked away, as if checking to see if anyone was eavesdropping. Then he looked back to Hank, and he whispered, "I think it may have been God."

"It sure could have been," Hank nodded.

"Really? I thought you'd blow that off immediately. You really think it could have been God?"

"I think it's definitely worth exploring."

"So, you don't think I'm crazy?" Strapp asked.

"Nah, you're not crazy. I hear him all the time."

"You do?"

"I do. But that's another story for another day. Let's talk about what he's saying to *you*."

Strapp opened his palms. "I got nothing, Hank."

"*Now you know how I feel.* Think about it, Strapp. Einstein once said, 'We cannot solve our problems with the same level of thinking that created them.' You're looking at this problem at eye level, and I think what you really need is a shift in perspective. We have got to think bigger. Step back. See it differently."

"Where do I even begin?"

Hank glanced to the table where a folded table tent advertised the coffee shop's loyalty program. Underneath it was a notebook and a pen that Hank had placed there before Strapp arrived. "This seems like the right time to give these to you."

He nudged the notebook toward Strapp.

"What's this?"

"Just a notebook and a pen. A journal, if you will."

"Whose is it?"

Strapp felt for a moment like it could be something from his father, and he wasn't sure he had the emotional capacity to process the living and breathing sight of his dad's handwriting.

"Don't worry, I'm not throwing you any curve balls. It's an empty notebook. All the pages are blank. It's for you."

Strapp nudged the book toward Hank. "I'm not a writer."

Hank inched it toward Strapp again. "You don't have to be. But there is a lot brewing in you, and I'd love to help you sort it out. I'm asking you to try something."

"What am I supposed to do?"

"I think the blank page could be a good place for you to sort through some of the things you're thinking, recalling, and questioning."

"The blank page is intimidating," Strapp said.

"Then go ahead and write something in it right now. That way it won't be quite so intimidating. Or empty."

Strapp leaned back in his chair, folding his arms. "I don't know if I feel like writing right now."

Hank leaned forward, toward Strapp. "Just open to the first page."

The two men maintained eye contact. Strapp wasn't interested, but Hank wasn't backing down.

Strapp exhaled a long, slow breath through his nose. His jaw tightened. He looked at Hank, and he picked up the pen.

"Atta' boy," Hank said, his eyes twinkling.

Strapp opened to the first page. "What am I supposed to write?"

"Anything."

Strapp exhaled again, this time fast and sharp. He scrawled his signature across the open page, and he set down the pen. He looked back at Hank.

"There you go. Own it. Own this notebook. Excellent choice."

Strapp looked away and his jaw tightened again. "What are we doing here, Hank?"

"Strapp, I'd like to mentor you."

"Mentor."

"Yes, sir. I'd like to teach you some things I know. And I'd like to begin with some things you may have wrong."

It all felt a little too vulnerable suddenly, with the notebook, the pages, and now suggestions of a list of things he had wrong—this was not a topic he enjoyed exploring. Hank pressed into the silence.

"Strapp, I've coached and mentored many, many men over the years—including your dad. When I see despair on a man's face, especially to the degree that I see on yours, the root is almost always a misunderstanding of God's character."

Strapp listened.

"There may be some 'mis-think' going on in that mind of yours."

"Mis-think?" Strapp said.

"We don't know what we don't know, Strapp. And sometimes, what we *think* we know is a little misguided. Let me ask you, who has taught you about God?"

"A lot of people. My parents, especially my dad. I made the decision to follow Christ when I was a kid. And my basketball coach in college, he was pretty important to me. He taught me a lot. I'm in church most Sundays."

"I'm so thankful for that, Strapp. More than you know. And some people think that making a decision to follow Jesus means they automatically get a download of robotic understanding; like because they've said *yes*, they now get who he is."

"Isn't it God's job to show me who he is?"

"Perhaps, yes. But we don't necessarily absorb who he is as we sit in church or open a Bible. Strapp, how much effort have you put into enriching your understanding of him?"

Strapp raised his eyebrows and opened his hands. Hank made a solid point, whether he wanted to admit it or not. "I mean, I don't know what I don't know. You're right about that."

"So, let's think about what you do know. Turn to a new page, and at the top, I want you to write '*God, I think you are...*'"

Strapp looked at him hesitantly.

"Come on, man. You have nothing to lose."

Strapp turned the page, wrote the words, and looked at the page.

"Now," Hank said, "What's the first thing that comes to mind?"

"Good. I think he is good," Strapp answered.

"Amen. I do, too. Write it down."

Strapp's pen made a scratching sound across the thick page.

He looked at Hank. Hank queried, "What else?"

"I keep going?"

"Sure. Let's see what comes to mind."

Strapp wrote.

In Charge.

Judge.

Powerful.

Loving.

He thought of the voice he heard in the bathroom. He wrote *In my head.*

He paused, his pen hovering in the air.

Then he wrote *Distant.*

He crossed it out.

"Why'd you cross it out?"

"It doesn't make sense," Strapp said.

"Say more about that."

"Well, because I just wrote that he's *in my head*—but I didn't mean he's a figment of my imagination, I meant that he's in my thoughts. So then how can I write that he's *distant?* How can he be both?"

"He can be both if it feels that way to you. You're a human being trying to make sense of an infinite God, and it's okay if you think of words that feel opposite from each other."

Strapp looked down at his page. He wrote, *Everywhere.*

All knowing.

Shepherd.

Forgiving.

Father.

Suddenly, his eyes welled with tears. He hadn't expected them.

Strapp lowered his head, struck once again with the grief of losing his dad so many years ago. This was all so hard and so palpable, this searing pain of loving and raising a son, all without the guidance of his father.

Hank put a warm, strong hand on Strapp's arm.

"Strapp, I know you miss him. I know, pal. What a good man he was—and he would love seeing the man you've become. I see so much of him in you."

Again, Hank let Strapp sit in the silence. Hank was comfortable with silence, and he never filled it without an invitation.

Finally, Strapp said, "It's why I called you. I needed to be near somebody who knew my dad. And I know how he loved you. He always said you were the wisest man he ever knew."

"We had an important relationship, your dad and me."

Strapp looked at Hank, his eyes wet with tears. "Will you help me?"

Hank reached across the table and put a hand on each of Strapp's shoulders. "I thought you'd never ask, Strapp. I'd love to join you on your journey, and I have a few things to show you. If you're in, then I'm all yours."

He extended his hand toward Strapp, inviting him to shake it. Strapp shook Hank's hand agreeably. "I'm in."

Hank's eyes seemed to sparkle with an idea. "I'd like to take you to some places to teach you a new perspective. It may seem strange and disconnected sometimes, but I think it'll all come together in the end." He pulled his car keys out of his pocket and showed them to Strapp. "Whaddya say? Do you have some time?"

"Right now?" Strapp looked at his watch. "Sure, I guess so."

"Good. I have an idea. Grab your notebook and jump in my truck. I have something I want to show you. But first, let's grab another cup of coffee for the road."

CHAPTER 9

Strapp kept stride with Hank as they left the coffee shop and headed into the parking lot. Hank's pickup truck had a Colorado bumper sticker that touted *Native*, and a pine-scented air freshener dangled from his rearview mirror. As Hank turned the key, Strapp recognized a few bars of the Eagles' "Peaceful, Easy Feeling."

Hank backed out of his parking space as Strapp said, "So, is there a name for this new situation going on with Joe?"

"Well, it's very normal, if that's what you're asking," Hank said.

"Is there a book I can read to figure out what to do next?"

Hank's head rolled back with kind laughter. "Yes, Strapp. This affliction could be called the Orphan's Spirit, and it shows up all throughout the Bible."

"Wait. What? I was talking about parenting books and adoption classes—something I can read or watch or study. I need you to show me what other parents have done."

"I'd be happy to show you, Strapp."

"I mean, is this something that surfaces a lot in adopted kids?"

"Strapp, man, I don't feel like you're hearing me. The Orphan's Spirit shows up in all of us."

"All of us? But I'm not an orphan. You knew my dad."

"Strapp, I have something I learned a very long time ago that I think will be helpful to you. I learned long ago that you can't take someone to a place where you haven't yet been yourself."

Strapp looked out the window to the open road. He waited for Hank to say more.

"In other words, Strapp, you can't teach Joseph what it means to be a son until you learn to be a son yourself."

"To be a son? That's something to learn?"

"You bet it is, Strapp. In fact, everything hangs in the balance of that lesson, I'd say."

"I thought a *son* is a title. It's what you are. Somebody's son," Strapp said.

"It's a word that exists in a relationship. In order to be a son, you need to recognize that you have a father."

Strapp shook his head. "I feel like you're speaking in code, Hank."

Hank laughed again. "If you want help, Strapp, I can teach you how to get to there, so to speak."

Strapp chuckled, rolling down his window. He put one arm out in the breeze, and with a huge sigh, he said, "Show me the way, Hank."

• • •

Early evening had set in by the time Strapp and Hank arrived at the horse barn. They took a seat on a bench near the arena. "This is one of my favorite spots, Strapp. I love this ranch. They train colts and fillies here; some of them go on to be therapy horses, and others run in races. I love to stop in and see who they're excited about. These horses were born for greatness, Strapp. They just don't know it yet."

"Born for greatness… what must that be like?"

Hank pointed out into the field, wordlessly guiding Strapp's view into the distance to see a brown and white horse inside a ring. Next to the young horse was a horse trainer, a strong young cowboy holding a rope in his hand. The horse paced in circles around him.

"Is that a wild horse, Hank?"

"It is. He's a colt, just a couple of years old. His name is Shakespeare."

Strapp laughed. "Great name. What's the cowboy trying to do?"

"Well, he's trying to teach Shakespeare to listen to him, maybe accept the reins or even the saddle." Just as Hank said that, Shakespeare bucked and raced laps around the pen.

"It's almost like he heard you. Doesn't look like the horse likes that idea," Strapp said.

"Most of them don't, no. See, Shakespeare thinks the trainer is trying to take something from him, and he feels like he's about to lose his freedom."

"Isn't he, though? Put reins on that horse and then he must obey. That hardly feels like freedom."

"But without reins on him, he runs wild. He may be free to make his own choices, but he'll never become who he could be, who he was made to be. Shakespeare thinks he wants to be wild and free, but he doesn't know who he is yet. There are gifts within him, there are experiences waiting for him, and there is a whole new life that could be his—possibilities he cannot even imagine—if he can learn to listen to his trainer. The cowboy is inviting him to listen."

Shakespeare stopped running, and the trainer came to stand beside the colt. He began to gently pet the horse, stroking his mane. Strapp could see him talking softly to Shakespeare as he touched him with the back of his hand. And then, in a swift and gentle move of an experienced trainer, the cowboy slipped a rope around the horse's neck.

"Well, would you look at that…" Strapp whispered.

With a loose and gentle rope around his neck, the horse began to follow the trainer. He stopped racing, stopped running, stopped pulling.

"How'd that happen so fast, Hank?"

"Oh, buddy, they're not finished. That's just the first step. The horse is filled with questions right now, wondering what kind of a situation he has just agreed to."

Strapp laughed. "I hear you, Shakespeare. Me, too."

"But look at him. Watch him." They watched as Shakespeare took a few steps with his trainer. "That horse seems to *want* to learn."

Strapp smiled. "Yep. Me, too."

"Shakespeare is about to realize that he was born for so much more. He was born to run, but he must learn to obey. His instinct is to live wild, but he has to learn how to trust the one who's training him."

Strapp and Hank watched as the trainer walked beside the horse, raising his knee alongside the horse's chest, comforting him with a quiet, gentle voice. They walked together, side by side, the cowboy talking and the horse listening.

As he talked to the colt, he put a bridle in his mouth, and the men watched as Shakespeare waved his head around in opposition. The cowboy let him wave his head, let him explore his options, and kept talking to him gently. With slow patience and a gentle voice, he put a halter on the horse. The men watched as he climbed onto Shakespeare, laying across the horse's back with his feet hanging down one side. After a few minutes in this position, the cowboy swung one of his legs over, and they watched as he positioned himself astride the horse's bare back. He rode him around the ring.

"Amazing," Strapp whispered.

"He's a smart boy, that horse. He just didn't know what he was created for."

Strapp spoke into the silence. "Shakespeare reminds me a lot of Joseph," Strapp said.

"I was hoping you might see that. Shakespeare is acting like he's all alone in the world, like he must fight to win, like everything is a battle and he can't trust anybody. He thinks he's better off on his own. Shakespeare is behaving like an orphan."

Strapp kept his eyes on Shakespeare as he let the words sink in.

Hank continued. "Joe has lived a lot of years on his own, and that's the life he knows best. He doesn't trust you and Julie yet. He doesn't trust this new life any more than Shakespeare trusts those reins around his neck."

Strapp looked at Shakespeare and folded his arms.

Hank's voice got lower. "Strapp, I know you see the parallels between Shakespeare and Joe… does the horse remind you of anyone else?"

Strapp's brow furrowed. "I'm not tracking."

Hank elbows him. "That colt reminds me a lot of *you*."

"What? Me?"

Strapp's jaw tightened.

"Let me ask you a different question, Strapp. How do you define meekness? What do you think of when I say that word?"

Strapp scoffed. "Well, I'd say *meek* sounds like *weak*."

"So, you'd say it's a bad thing?" Hank asked.

Hank pointed back to the horse barn, and the two men walked together. Strapp put his hands in the pockets of his jeans. "It's not very masculine, that's for sure. What kind of a man lets people walk all over him? No way. It's passive. Negative."

"So, you wouldn't want anyone to describe you as 'meek,' then?"

Strapp scoffed again and shook his head. "No, thanks."

"It might surprise you to know what it really means. The actual definition is *bridled power*."

Strapp did a double take. "Bridled?"

Hank nodded. "Yes, sir. Strength under control."

"I thought it meant you're a doormat."

Hank smiled. "Most people think that. But it's quite the opposite. Meekness is very much a sign of strength. A meek person is humble, teachable, and patient under suffering."

"Under *suffering*? I think that's about the last time I'd be patient."

"You're in a season of suffering right now, Strapp."

"And I'm not feeling very patient. I want you to fix this. All of it."

"We're working on it, Strapp. Stay with me. The word 'meek' means *becoming used to the hand.*"

"You're some kind of a walking dictionary, Hank."

Hank laughed. "I guess I've collected a lot of words over time."

"Words *and* wisdom," Strapp said. "Tell me about this business of 'getting used to the hand.'"

Hank pointed out to the horse field. "Well, look again at Shakespeare. See what the cowboy does? He's walking gently, letting the horse get used to him in every way. First with his hand, then with the rope, then with the halter, bridle, saddle. That mighty creation is learning to tame his strength."

Strapp shook his head, deep in thought. "Man, Hank."

"God created you for greatness, son. He didn't create you to be ruled by your instincts, and he didn't create you to be a slave to your ideas, desires, or even to anyone else. He created you for greatness. Joseph, too."

They walked together into the horse barn. "Now let me show you another one of my favorites, Strapp." Hank pointed to a strong black stallion. "See this horse? His name is Duke."

"Another great name."

"Right? I love that name. Duke is training to become a world-class racehorse."

"Like, the Triple Crown kind of races?"

"Oh, maybe someday, who knows? For now, he's running in local races—and he's winning."

"No kidding?"

"No kidding. This horse was born with an incredible, raw talent. He was predisposed for greatness. He could be the Michael Jordan of the horse racing world."

"Born to win," Strapp said, the hint of a smile on his face.

"Most athletes have that predisposition, don't you think? Let me ask you this: if you went out and shot baskets every day, if you worked out as hard as you could, how long do you think it would take for you to be as good as Michael Jordan?"

Strapp laughs. "I think that would happen on the other side of never."

Hank pats him on the back. "And there's nothing wrong with that reality. That man was born with a certain giftedness, right?"

"Sure. Like you said, he was born to win."

"But he still had to learn what to do with that greatness, right? So, think about Duke, here. At his core, Duke is a wild horse. It's not that long ago that he was flailing about like Shakespeare. Duke wasn't born knowing how to win. He was born with no direction, and no understanding of what to do with all that energy—he had to learn how to channel all that power. Imagine if they put a jockey on Duke and put him in a race when he still had a mind and will like Shakespeare, back when he was a colt with no training."

"I wouldn't want to be that jockey."

"Right? Duke would have the power and the ability, but no direction. He *became used to the hand* of his trainer. He learned over time that if he submits and surrenders to this discipline and the training, then he could become a winning horse."

"You're telling me Duke is *meek*?"

"That's exactly what he is. He knows how strong he is, but he *chooses* to be gentle. He is the very example of bridled power."

"How does a person become meek?"

"You first have to recognize whose you are."

"Who I am?" Strapp asked.

"No. *Whose*. You must first see that this life isn't about you. It's not easy, and it doesn't feel good. But the moment you realize that you are wild in your core, that God wants to discipline you and give you purpose and focus – until you get to that point, you have no chance at meekness. You can't become meek without first realizing there is one to whom you belong. When a horse submits to the bridle and the bit, he positions himself to win the race. His power becomes focused and directed."

"Controlled strength."

"Yes, sir. Now Duke can run with purpose because he knows where his master wants him to go."

"How do I do it, Hank? Tell me what to do."

"It comes down to three things, brother." Hank counted out on three fingers, "Tame the temper, calm the passions, and manage the impulses of the heart."

Strapp laughed. "Just those three? You make it sound so easy."

"Well, look at them one at a time. When a wild horse is bridled, tamed, and disciplined, its power becomes more focused and directed, more controlled and strengthened. Now it can run with purpose."

"I hear you, Hank. I think it's about realizing where your power comes from."

"You got it, pal. Look at Jesus. Jesus knew whose he was, and he knew who he was. That's how he functioned and operated. At any point, he could have called down a legion of angels to take out those who were trying to arrest him. He could have spoken a word and been taken off the cross. He had the power to do anything he chose to do, but he chose to submit."

"Not with weakness, but with meekness," Strapp said.

"Strapp, Jesus knew what he had been called to do. He surrendered to the authority of his father and he chose to walk in sonship. That's where the power is, my friend."

Strapp listened. He petted Duke's mane. "What do I do about Joseph?"

"Well, there are lots of ways to train a wild stallion, Strapp. Other trainers might wrestle him into submission, wrangle him under control. But that doesn't mean the horse would trust him. He might obey because he's afraid, not because he respects his trainer."

"So, I need to earn his trust," Strapp said.

"Just like the cowboy with the colt. Be patient."

As the two men turned to walk back to Hank's truck, they heard a commotion behind them. Strapp looked back to watch as Shakespeare lowered his head, raised his hindquarters into the air, and kicked out with his hind legs. The horse bucked the cowboy to the ground.

"Hank! Did you see that?"

"Yes, sir. It's Shakespeare's instinct as a wild horse. All a natural part of the process."

Shakespeare ran in circles in the ring. The cowboy waited for him to slow, and then he approached Shakespeare as he had before—with slow patience and a gentle voice.

"So, they begin again?" Strapp asked.

"Over and over. It's a long process, and it won't be easy on either of them."

When Strapp opened the door to Hank's truck, he saw the notebook lying on the seat where he had left it.

Hank said, "Remember, Strapp, Joe still thinks he is an orphan. He still has an orphan's spirit, and he believes he's on his own in the world. Be consistent. Show him who you are. Show him you're there, you're with him, and you love him. Don't try to overpower him—

that'll never work. Just be beside him. Let him hear your voice in the good and the bad. He'll become used to your hand."

Strapp opened the notebook. He wrote down, "Tame the temper."

Hank added, "Calm the passions."

Strapp wrote it down, and then he said slowly as he wrote, "And manage the impulses of the heart."

Hank said, "You and Joe."

Strapp wrote, *Me and My Boy.*

CHAPTER 10

"Caroline and Joseph, time for dinner!" Julie called up the stairs to their bedrooms. She spooned the baked beans from the crockpot to the serving bowl, and she gave the salad one last toss before carrying everything to the table.

Strapp collected the bratwursts off the grill, placed them on a platter, and turned off the gas. Strapp closed the sliding door and set the platter on the table. "All set," he said.

"Thanks for grilling, babe."

"Anytime."

Caroline took her spot at the table. "Bratwurst—yum. Must be almost summertime."

"Right?" Julie said as she sat down, unfolding her napkin onto her lap. "Seemed like a good night for a meal like this. I think Joe will be excited about this meal, too. When we were at the grocery store, he seemed especially interested in the beans."

He had strolled the aisles with her, and when they came to the cans of soups and vegetables, he stopped walking. He stood still, staring at the cans of beans. He reached out one hand and touched the copper label.

"Do you like those, Joe? Would you like for me to fix them sometime?"

As if he hadn't heard her, Joe's hand dropped to his side and he walked ahead without answering. He had been with their family for over a year now, but still, the journey of learning what her son liked and disliked sometimes felt like piecing together a complicated flower arrangement, combining different colors and varieties to see what made him smile. The beans seemed like a clue. She followed behind him and put the can into her cart, making a mental note to grab bratwurst and buns, planning her menu.

"Joseph?" she called again.

"Joe, come on down, buddy," Strapp added.

"I'm coming, I'm coming," Joe said, as he bounced into the dining room. He settled into his chair and reached for the buns.

"Ah, one minute, pal," Julie said, reaching for his hand. "Remember, we need to thank the Lord for our food."

"Oh, yeah. Sorry," Joe said, putting his hands in his lap, as they had taught him to do. He bowed his head and closed his eyes as Strapp thanked the Lord for their meal.

They passed the brats and buns around the table, each serving themselves and chatting about the day. Julie served beans to each person since the bowl was hot. She lifted a scoop for Joe, but before the beans spilled out onto his plate, his hand lashed out and hit the spoon. His fist sent the beans flying across the room. They made a splatting noise as they hit the wall.

Julie gasped.

"Joe! Joseph!" Strapp said. He grabbed Joe's wrist.

"No," Joe said, pulling his wrist away and reaching for his plate. "No. No!"

Joe picked up his bratwurst and threw it at Strapp's face. He threw his plate onto the floor.

Caroline ducked.

Julie froze.

Joe looked at Julie with fire in his eyes. "You *bitch.*"

"Excuse me?" Julie said. "What did you just say?"

"I said you are a bitch," he spat at her.

"Don't you ever call me that again, Joseph. Do you hear me?"

"Yeah? And what are you going to do about it?"

"I'll start by taking away your Gameboy and your PlayStation. Starting now."

"I hate you! I hate this stupid family! I don't even know why I'm here—you don't want me, and I don't want to be here!"

"Don't even go there, Joe," Julie said. "I am sick and tired of your temper tantrums! It really pisses me off that we can't even have a nice dinner as a family anymore."

Joe lunged at Julie, knocking the spoon out of her hand and nearly toppling her backward in her chair. Strapp dove across the table and intercepted his son. He restrained him before Joe could hit Julie or Caroline. He spoke evenly and sternly, but loudly. "Son, that is *enough.*"

"*You* are enough!" His words didn't even make sense, but that's how it was when Joe flew into a rage. His words were illogical and irrational, and his violence was imminent. Joe pulled from Strapp and ran from the table. He raced up the stairs. They listened as his bedroom door slammed.

"What happened? What was that about?" Caroline asked.

Julie said, "The beans."

She suddenly remembered the photos and the stories his social worker had shared with them about Joe's early years. All alone in the house, Joe had gotten hungry. He found a can of beans on a shelf in the kitchen, and he tried and tried to twist it open. He had no understanding of a can opener, or how the can might open differently than a jar. He had been so hungry, but he couldn't get to the food.

When Julie had seen him linger over the can in the grocery store, she had thought he was remembering something he liked, something he wanted. She had no idea that he was recalling a buried and painful memory that maybe even he couldn't fully recall.

Joe remembered being home alone and so hungry. He had smashed a can of beans onto the floor, trying to break it open.

"Trauma trigger," Strapp said to Julie.

She nodded and put her hand over her mouth. "I would never have…"

"I know, babe. I know. We are all learning," Strapp said.

He looked to Caroline, trying to explain. "Honey, sometimes a smell or a taste can bring back a bad memory for Joe. Something bad must have happened to him a long time ago, and he just remembered it."

Caroline looked back and forth between her parents. “Do we go help him? What do we do?” she asked.

“I’ll go,” Strapp said, getting up from the table.

He kissed Julie’s forehead and went up to Joe’s room.

• • •

Strapp knocked on Joe’s bedroom door, not to ask permission, but to let him know he was coming in. “Joe?” he said, peering around the open door.

The bed was empty. The floor was strewn with Legos. Joe wasn’t anywhere to be found. Strapp took a few more steps into the room, and then he opened the closet door. There sat Joe, facing a dark corner inside his closet.

“Hey, pal,” he said, gently. He got on his knees, then sat down on the floor. “It’s okay, buddy. I’m here.”

“No,” Joe said.

“I know, son.”

He sat silent and still next to his son. He would sit there all evening if Joe needed.

Joe sat still, staring into the corner, his back to Strapp. Joe’s hands were clenched in fists, and his forearms trembled with the tension.

“It’s okay, pal. Take a breath.” Strapp audibly breathed in and out, waiting for Joe’s shoulders to relax, for his forearms to relax, for his hands to open.

A few minutes passed. He heard a small shuffle in the hallway, and he looked up to see Julie standing in the doorway of Joe’s room. Their eyes met, and she raised her eyebrows, wordlessly asking if Joe was okay. Strapp nodded, and then he breathed in and out again, letting Joe listen to his calm steadiness.

Strapp nodded his head in the direction of the stairs, wordlessly asking if the bean situation had been taken care of. Julie nodded. She held his gaze, put her hand to her heart, and then she went back downstairs.

After a long silence, Joe said so softly, "Sorry."

"It's okay, Joe. Everything is okay."

"There's a mess."

"Messes can be fixed, son. It's okay."

"Beans," Joe said.

"They're cleaned up," Strapp said. "No more beans."

Joe's shoulders relaxed a little more.

Strapp said, "How about a peanut butter sandwich?"

Joe nodded.

Strapp knew not to startle his son. "Let's go make you a sandwich, buddy."

Joe looked over his shoulder, first at the floor, and then up to Strapp's face. His eyes pleaded.

Strapp opened his hand and held it out to his son.

"You don't have to be hungry anymore, son. Let's get you some food."

CHAPTER 11

Hank and Strapp met for lunch at a sports bar. They ordered a couple of burgers with fries. Hank said, "Tell me, Strapp. What is God teaching you these days?"

Strapp dipped his fry in some ketchup and took a bite. "Oh, man, where to even begin… we have had some bumps in the road. There are some trauma triggers that we know to expect now, but some things jump out at us without any warning."

He told Hank about some of the scenes in their home; at the table, on the basketball court. "We got a call from the school this week, and Julie and I had to go meet with Joe's teacher and the principal."

"What happened?"

"Joe hit somebody in his classroom. Nobody knew why, but they were in line for lunch and Joe hit this kid in the face with his lunchbox."

"Unprovoked? He just hauled off and hit him?"

"Well, that's what we had thought, and that's what it looked like. But here's what we're learning, Hank—when Joe is triggered, it's like something shuts down in his brain. I mean, if you watch him in that moment, his eyes look empty. There's this disconnect; like he can't think about what he's doing. Like he doesn't even know what he's doing until after the fact."

"But something must have triggered him in that lunch line, right?"

"Here's the thing, Hank. In the moment, nobody could tell us what happened. But we later learned that he was defending a girl in the class. Her mother called the teacher, and she said that this boy had been making fun of her daughter. The teacher did some investigating, and we learned that the boy was picking on her, and Joe had stepped in."

"With the lunchbox."

"I mean, it's not ideal, but he has a huge heart, Hank."

"I have no doubt about that."

"He's a protector. And I'll tell you this, I love listening to Joe pray. That boy knows how to talk to God."

"Yeah? Tell me more about that."

"He knows a lot about the Bible, about God, and how to pray. Somebody has invested in him, teaching him the right things; it kind of blows me away. A lot of kids his age will say memorized prayers, like little poems, you know. Even some adults only ever say The Lord's Prayer, but Joe talks to God like he knows him."

"Let me ask you, would you like to have Joseph and Caroline say the same thing to you every day?"

"No way, I don't need memorized words."

"You would like to know what's really on their minds, right?"

"Any good father would want to know," Strapp said.

"Right. You want to hear the heart of your child, and that's how God is. He doesn't want memorized words, Strapp, he wants what is on your heart. When Jesus said, 'Pray this way,' he was modeling a heart posture and an attitude, he wasn't telling you what to say. Are there times when you just let yourself talk to him?"

"Yes, but it is usually when I am praying and asking God to fight against the enemy. It's in moments when I know that Satan is trying to wreck my life, and I need help. But even then, I'm not always sure what to pray. I just kind of cry out to him," Strapp said.

"I hear you. A lot of people think that way too, but what if you thought of it in an entirely different way? Have you ever been in court? Ever have to appear before a judge for anything?"

"Sure, we went to family court when we adopted Joe."

"Excellent example. So, what if I suggested that the Lord's Prayer—again, a model, not a script—is more like a framework for approaching a judge?"

"So, then what am I supposed to say?"

"Well, let's break it down. What's the first phrase?"

Strapp recalls from memory. "Our Father, who art in heaven."

"Okay, stop right there. Let's just focus on those words and embrace what Jesus is saying. First and foremost, as you approach this Judge, recognize who you're talking to. Recognize whose presence you're in. Don't just rush in with disrespect like a spoiled kid or you'll be cast out of the courtroom faster than you came in."

"I thought God just wanted us to be in his presence. You just said he wants to know what's on my mind."

"He does, Strapp. Oh, he sure does. But he demands respect and healthy fear. We must never forget that he is the Great I Am. Recognize that he's your Father."

"So, which is it? Father or Judge?"

"Yes."

Strapp began to chuckle a bit to himself. "You crack me up, Hank."

"How is that?"

"You just remind me of Yoda sometimes. I'm sorry. Please go on. This is a lot to hold."

"Well, look again at the words Jesus said. He didn't begin the prayer with 'Our Judge, who is in heaven.' He said, 'Our Father.' I don't think that was by chance at all. He chose his words very carefully. It's your Father who has chosen you. He wants relationship with you. If anybody has favor, it's *you*."

"That's a relief."

"But he cannot be in the presence of sin."

"Then I don't stand a chance," Strapp said. "I keep feeling like I take one step toward learning, only to take a step right back to not understanding."

"Here's the deal, Strapp. Your father is in heaven, and you're not. He is perfect, and you're not. He has perspective that you don't have, and he has an authority and a power that you don't have."

"So how do I stand a chance? How does anyone stand a chance? How can anyone even approach God?"

"By throwing yourself to the feet of the judge and his ruling. You begin by acknowledging that you are not in a position to demand anything. This judge is your father, he's in heaven, and he's the holiest king. No one is greater than he. Start by remembering that. Do you have your notebook with you?"

"Sure do!" Strapp said, pulling the black notebook and a pen from his messenger bag.

"Let's jot a few things down."

Strapp opened the notebook and uncapped his pen. "What do you want me to write down?"

"Let's see if we can explore this formula for prayer. Tell me again how the prayer began."

"Okay. Our Father, who art in heaven, hallowed be your name."

"But what does that mean?"

"I'm supposed to remember who I'm talking to. Remember that he's a holy, righteous judge."

"Yes, sir. Write that down."

Strapp wrote in his notebook:

How to Pray.

Approach with Respect.

Hank said, "What comes next?"

Strapp recalled more from memory. "Your kingdom come, your will be done, on earth as it is in heaven."

"What do you hear there, Strapp?"

"I hear Jesus asking God to make it the same on earth as it is in heaven."

"Yes, and Jesus is saying, 'I'm about to bring my requests to you, but first of all, I want to be clear: this is not about what I want. I trust whatever you decide.'"

Strapp adds, "So it's like saying, 'I'm about to ask for something, but before I do, I know you have the power to say no.'"

"Yes! Write that down."

Strapp wrote, *Not my will. Yours.*

He said, "This makes sense. I mean, as a father, I want to do what's best for my kids, but I also want to know what they're longing for."

"Even if they're way off base, even if they're asking for something ridiculous?"

Strapp nodded. "Even if it's never going to happen."

He tapped his pen on the notebook.

Hank said, "What does Jesus say next?"

"Let's see. Then he says, 'Give us today our daily bread.' I hear Provider in those words."

"Yes. What has he provided?"

"Um, everything."

"Everything. Your wisdom, your creativity, your cleverness, your business acumen—you might think that these traits have given you the ability to provide for your family. But God is the one who not only gives wealth—he gives even the ability to generate wealth."

Strapp gestures an explosion in his thoughts: mind blown. "It's all from him."

"And in this part of the prayer, you're trusting him for whatever is next. Your next meal, next idea, next breath."

Strapp wrote down, *Trust him to provide.*

Then he asked, "What is that part about trespassing? 'Forgive us our trespasses as we forgive those who trespass against us.'"

"Well, before you can receive forgiveness for yourself, you must first examine your heart. Jesus is outlining a conscious process that says we need to inspect our own heart and resolve any issues with anyone else."

"Is this all part of approaching God?"

"Before you ask for anything at all. Yes. Jesus models for us the way to cover all our bases, so you can come before a holy Father, a holy King, and make your requests. For the measure you choose to forgive others will also be given to you."

The pen mindfully scribbled *Forgive.*

Strapp continued, "And then, 'Deliver us from evil.'"

"Ah, yes. Temptation. The Bible is clear that God will test us. Do you remember when Jesus was in the desert for forty days and Satan tempted him?"

"Of course."

"Well, do you know who led Jesus into the desert to be tested through this temptation?"

"Satan?"

"Most people would think that, but that is incorrect. Scripture said that the Spirit led him into the desert to be tempted."

"His own father?"

"Yes, his own Father led him into the desert, knowing what Jesus would have to go through. God knew that Jesus needed to overcome the temptation of the enemy before he could carry out his purpose. In this part of the prayer, you're asking God to bring forth any areas in your life that he knows to be broken. Any areas of sin, and any tendencies toward sin, so you can fulfill your purpose as well."

Strapp chuckled. "That could be a long list."

"It sure could. And Jesus is showing us how to place those before God, how to pray that those temptations may be thwarted. That is how you resist the enemy, by submitting to God. Then the enemy will have no option but to flee."

"At what point can I present my request to God? When can I ask for what I need?"

"Well, now that you've followed Jesus' model, you've prayed the way he taught us to pray. Now you've positioned yourself to share your requests."

Strapp laughed. "Finally."

He wrote down, *Now Ask*.

"That's sonship. The Father wants to manifest these promises in your life, or he wouldn't have made them in the first place. But he cannot grant those promises to you if you're not walking in sonship."

"So, it's not a battlefield issue. It's an identity issue."

"Now you're talking, Strapp. This is how you enter the presence of God, who has all authority. Jesus is saying, 'let me teach you how to walk in power and authority.' For the prayer of a righteous man—that's a prayer God answers."

"So, it's not about how badly I want it?"

"No, everybody wants something badly, for probably good reasons. It's the righteousness that makes the difference."

"And by praying this way, I'm setting myself up for God to say 'yes'?"

"It's about having a relationship with your Father. Jesus is saying, I will teach you how to be righteous as you step into the presence of the Ancient of Days. You're asking for something, and God wants to say yes."

"I've never thought about any of this, not in this way."

"See, Strapp, sonship is about intimacy. When you talk to God, you're exercising your intimacy. You are tapping into your inheritance through the gift of the Father. We think we have to earn it, say the right things, do the right things in order to earn his protection and blessings. We'll even follow a script if it seems like it will work. But he just wants to have a conversation with you. He's asking us to just be with Him."

"Just be," Strapp said.

"Just be," Hank told him.

Strapp looked at the words on his page.

How to pray.

Approach with respect.

Not my will.

Trust him to Provide.

Need forgiveness. Forgive others.

Now Ask.

Just Be.

Hank said, "You see, Strapp, there are all these things concealed in Heaven, and God wants to give them to you. He wants to give them to all His children. Things He destined for us to have. When you are positioned and aligned, the things of heaven can manifest through you."

"Hank, what are those things?"

"Well, it's everything that you can think of that relates to the characteristics of God. It's love, joy, peace, patience—it's miracles. He wants to manifest those things through you. He could do it any other way, but he wants to manifest his hands, his feet, his love, his kindness, his goodness, his miracles, his healing—he wants to manifest those through you. He just wants you to position yourself. Position yourself in a relationship with Jesus, so these things may flow through you."

"Like a conduit."

"A conduit. Yes, I think I see where you are going. Tell me more, Strapp."

"Well, my dad was an electrician, and I remember going with him to work a few times, back when I thought I'd learn the trade from him. I don't remember very much, but I remember asking him to connect the dots for me. 'There's this electrical box on the outside, and somehow that box makes the lights turn on inside the building?' I remember he taught me the word 'conduit.' The conduit carries the power from here to there."

"The conduit in and of itself isn't special, right, Strapp?"

"Right—it just carries the power from here to there," Strapp said.

"And as a son, God wants you to choose to position yourself in relationship with him so the power can move from there to here—so the things of Heaven can manifest here. The Lord's prayer ties into that. It's about positioning ourselves properly because the Father is not going to share his glory with just anyone. It requires us to be properly positioned. That's what the Lord's prayer is all about: positioning."

"Positioning?" Strapp asked.

Hank smiled. "I think you're going to love this next place I'm taking you, Strapp." Hank waved to the server, asking for the check. Then he said, "Tell me, son. Do you like football?"

CHAPTER 12

Hank pulled his truck into the parking lot of the Denver Broncos training facility. Strapp saw a building large enough to be an airplane hangar, and he saw a football field with a whole lot of orange. "Denver Broncos?" Strapp said.

"I thought you might like to have a peek at a pre-season practice."

"Hank, are you kidding? Heck yeah, let's do this!"

Both men got out of the truck, and Strapp gave Hank a fist bump as they walk toward the field.

"I can't believe we're here. I've been curious to get a look at the newest draft pick for the Broncos," Strapp said.

"I am sure that is important, but I'd really like for you to see the offensive and defensive linemen. They're my favorite players on the field."

"The linemen? Watching the linemen is your favorite part of the game?"

"Definitely," Hank said, as they took their seats on the grass hill with the thousands of other Denver Broncos fans that came out to watch the first preseason practices of the season. "The action of the linemen is where it all happens. That's where everything falls into place."

"But what is there to watch?" Strapp asked. "It's just a bunch of big guys who are trying to keep the other big guys from getting in their way. There isn't much excitement in that."

"Sure," Hank nodded. "You—and almost every other football fan—focus on the ball. Everybody is enamored by the strong-armed quarterback, the powerful running backs, and the graceful, speedy receivers."

Strapp nodded. "Now you're talking."

"I know, I know. Everyone likes the game-changing plays, the great catches, the long runs and the big hits. But I'm going to let you in on a secret, Strapp. Those linemen are some of the greatest athletes on the planet. They are the best in the world at what they do. If the linemen don't do their job the right way, the rest of the team doesn't stand a chance."

"Okay, I'm intrigued. I didn't know you knew so much about football. Tell me more," Strapp said.

"Well, take a look at what they're doing right now," Hank said, as they settled onto the wet grass. "They're standing on the line of scrimmage, and they're going to spend a lot of time there."

"Why do they spend so much time being still? The play doesn't happen in the stillness. The play is what happens next."

"See, that's where you're wrong, big fella. The play is unfolding even before the center snaps the ball. Watch them—" he nudged Strapp and pointed to the players. "It looks like time stands still out there while they're all crouched on the line of scrimmage. But see the coaches? They're walking around them, telling them how to stand, where to put their feet, where to put their hands. They're working on balance and placement. They'll do these drills for hours on end."

"I thought you said these guys were the best athletes on the planet. This seems like basic fundamentals—seems like these guys should have learned it in flag football in fourth grade."

"That's the thing about fundamentals, Strapp. They become the foundation of who you are."

Strapp smiled. "I sense a metaphor."

"You're onto me, pal," Hank said. "This football field is filled with metaphors. Positioning is where it all begins. You want to know what it looks like to walk as a son? It all begins right here."

"It all begins… on the football field? I've got to hear this. Go on."

"Believe it or not, what you are watching right now is a metaphor for the battles of life."

Hank pointed again to the football field. Once again, the offense and defense line up against one another to begin a live scrimmage. Hank points Strapp's attention. "Take a look at what is about to happen in this drill. You see all of the players getting into position, and then—*snap!*"

The center snapped the ball to the quarterback, and chaos unfolded on the field.

"Did you see that?" Hank asked.

"It happened fast."

"Kind of like life, right?"

Strapp laughed. "Yes, Hank. Kind of like life."

"Think about this: these guys have been instructed on where to stand so they can be ready when the ball snaps. But they don't stand in the same place—they have to move and respond, right?"

"Fast."

"Exactly, just like—"

"Just like life." Strapp finished his sentence. "I'm picking up what you're putting down, Hank."

"When you're in relationship with Jesus, you're in position to receive his blessing, favor, and protection. And then life happens. And that's when you must make the next decision to stay in line with what he has called you to do. If you don't start in the right position, then you don't stand a chance when the bullets start flying. Or, in this case, the ball."

"So, what am I supposed to do if the bullets are already flying? I mean, Hank, this is great and all, but we are kind of post-snap at our house, so to speak. It's kind of late to learn where to stand now. I have to know what steps to take next."

"The good news is, you're already in right position. Do you remember the moment when you positioned yourself for sonship?"

"Are you talking about the moment I committed my life to Christ? Of course, I remember," Strapp said. "That is a night I will never forget. I was just a kid when I prayed to ask Christ to come into my life. I didn't know much, but I knew I needed God."

Hank smiled. "I remember that night, too. See, you recognized your need for a Father, and you positioned yourself to become his son. That's the first step. Whether you really knew it or not, in that moment when you recognized what Jesus did for you on the cross, you positioned yourself in the right place."

"And now it's time to realign."

"You got it, pal. You're in the middle of the play. I'm here to help you remember your fundamentals. Look—" Hank points to the field again, "another play."

The players come up to the line for the next play and Hank and Strapp focus their attention on the action. The QB takes the snap and drops back. His path is clear, protected by the linemen. He sinks down into his throwing position and delivers a perfect spiral 40 yards downfield to a wide receiver who has created separation from the defender. He brings in the perfectly thrown ball and strides effortlessly into the end zone for a touchdown.

Hank pumps his fist, "Now that is sonship!"

"Now that is *sonship*," Strapp smiles, shaking his head.

"All of the players began the play perfectly positioned. Once the ball was snapped, they realigned their formation to respond to whatever the defense was going to throw at them. That was beautiful. It all starts with the basic fundamentals. One day at a time, one play at a time. Positioning and alignment…the foundational characteristics of sonship. It's called righteousness."

Strapp opened his notebook. He wrote,

Positioning: On the Team.

Alignment: Executing the Play.

Then he wrote his next thoughts.

Real Life Positioning: I'm a son of God. This does not change.

Alignment: How will I respond to the chaos and challenges of life?

He looked at Hank. "Man, I have a lot to learn. You're still in this with me, right?" Strapp asked.

"I'm still in, Strapp."

CHAPTER 13

"Joe, what color would you like to be?" Caroline asked, lifting the lid off the game of *Sorry!*

"I want to be red," Joe said. He was ten years old now, and red had been his favorite color for all of a decade.

Caroline smiled. "I could have guessed that. Red it is. I'll be green, Mom is yellow, and Dad is blue."

Caroline and Joe placed all the pieces in the Start Circles, and Julie and Strapp joined them at the kitchen table. Tuesday evening was family game night, and *Sorry!* had become a family favorite. Every week, Caroline asked Joe what color he wanted to be, and every week he chose red.

"Mom gets to go first this time," Caroline said. Somehow, she had become the game master, setting up and remembering who had gone first each week.

"I wanted to go first," Joe said.

"You can go next, since you sit beside her."

Julie drew a 4.

Joe drew an 8.

Caroline drew a 2: she could move a piece onto the board, and she got to go again. Her next card was a 3, so she advanced her piece three spaces.

"You did that on purpose," Joe said.

"What do you mean? It was the next card, Joe."

"But you knew you'd go third, so you made that 2 the third card," Joe scowled.

"I did not, Joe. It's just how it happened. Remember? The tricky thing about the game of *Sorry!* is how to get your pieces out of the Start Circle. Not just any number will do, and you must draw a 1 or a 2 to send a guy out into the race around the board. You'll get a 1 or a 2 in a minute, I'm sure. Dad's turn."

"Come on, man," Strapp said, "Let's just play." Strapp drew a 5.

On Julie's turn, she drew an 11.

Joe drew a 7. He sighed loudly. He pounded his elbow on the table and put his chin in his hand.

Caroline drew a 1, so she moved another piece out of the circle and onto the board.

"You did it again!" Joe shouted.

"Joe, I'm not cheating."

"Oh, yeah, right! A 2 and *then* a 1?"

"Honey, she just got lucky. It's just how it goes sometimes," Julie said.

"For her! Everything works for her!"

Strapp said, "Joe, take a look, pal. I don't have any pieces out, and neither does Mom. Let's just keep playing, and everybody will have pieces in play soon."

Joe sighed again.

Strapp drew a 1. "There we go! That's what I'm talking about!" He dramatically moved his blue piece onto the board with a high arc and a grand entrance.

Julie drew a 2. "Oh, yay," she said, moving a piece out and drawing again. She drew an 8 and moved her piece forward.

Joe lunged for the deck of cards. He drew a 4. "I told you! I'll never get a piece on the board!" He folded his arms, slouching low in his chair.

"Joe," Caroline said, "You're being irrational. It's just a game." She turned over a 3 and advanced her piece.

"I hate this game. I never win."

Julie answered, "Sometimes you do. Two Tuesdays ago, you were the winner. Remember?

"Shut up," Joe said, furrowing his brow.

"Joseph," Strapp said, his voice stern. "That is enough."

Strapp turned over his next card, a 7.

Julie turned over a 4, and she moved her piece backward four spaces, as the card directed.

"I hate this family," Joe said in a low voice. His brows were furrowed in knots, and his arms were folded tight.

"You don't hate this family, Joe," Caroline said, "You're just mad because you didn't get a 1 or a 2!"

"You don't know how I feel!" Joe shouted.

Strapp and Julie each spoke at the same time to a different child. "Joe." "Caroline."

Both children answered at the same time, "What?!"

Julie said, "Okay, everybody. Time out. This is supposed to be *fun,* okay? Let's take a minute, take a breather, and gather ourselves."

Caroline folded her hands. Joe stared at her from beneath his eyebrows.

"You like her more than me," Joe said to his parents.

"Honey," Julie kept her voice even, fully aware of the escalation in the room. "No, we don't."

"Yes, you do. She was yours first."

Strapp said carefully, "She was in our family first, yes. But then we prayed for you, and we waited for you, and we looked for you, and we found you."

Joe's eyes focused on Caroline with laser precision.

In a gesture of making peace, Caroline put her hand out, palm up. "Hand Sandwich? Family first?"

She waited for someone to place their hand in hers, to follow through with the family tradition. But instead of putting his hand on top, Joe lashed out and slapped her open palm.

"Family *Never*!" he said.

Caroline gasped and pulled her hand back.

Julie placed her arms out between her two children, as a referee stopping a fight.

Strapp sensed the split-second before Joe stood to his feet, and he stood to stop him from whatever outburst would come next. But he didn't reach Joe fast enough.

Joe reached over to the bookshelf behind him, where Julie had displayed the gavel and the photos from his adoption day. Joe grabbed the gavel in his fist and threw it at the window.

Julie lunged toward the window. The move was based on instinct, and she couldn't be sure if she was trying to catch the gavel, or to stop the window from breaking, or to shield her family from the glass as it shattered.

Strapp reached for Joe. He knew the drill now; he needed to contain Joe from the dangerous threat of himself. He held Joe's forearms, and Joe kicked Strapp in the shin. Strapp moved with the stealth of a ninja—or at least as a parent who has learned to anticipate the moves of his child. As Joe's foot sank into his leg, Strapp leveraged his weight to move behind his son and restrain him. Joe thrashed in Strapp's arms, and he kicked his legs wildly, flipping the *Sorry!* board game.

The pieces flew through the air, landing in the broken glass on the floor.

• • •

The next morning after Caroline and Joe were in school, Julie finished folding a load of laundry. She stripped the sheets from each bed, and replaced them with a fresh, clean set. In Joe's room, she held the sheets to her face, breathing in the scent of her favorite fabric softener. Her heart felt broken. Everything was harder than she thought it would be, and it kept getting more difficult.

"Sometimes love is a decision. It's clean underwear and folded shirts. It's fresh sheets on the bed and cold milk in the fridge," she told herself. Love is about creating a home, and sometimes it manifests in the tasks of keeping a house—especially when her heart ran dry with fatigue, exhaustion, and worry. She was choosing to learn how to love this child, even when her heart wasn't in it.

When Julie lifted Joe's pillow, it felt heavy. From the outside of the pillowcase she felt lumps at the bottom. Something was in there. Some *things*.

When she reached inside the pillowcase, she discovered a secret collection: a handful of cheerios, some bites of cheese that had hardened, and some graham crackers that were soft with age. She found a pencil, and a framed picture of Strapp, Julie, and Caroline that was taken when Caroline was in preschool, when there were only three of them.

She found the bracelet Strapp had given her last Valentine's Day.

She found a red piece from the *Sorry!* game.

He had been collecting things. Maybe they were things he wanted to keep, remember, and stow away in case all of this could be taken away from him.

Julie struggled with a jumble of so many emotions, all at once. She felt compassion for this orphan who felt he needed to piece the world together for himself. She felt relieved to find her bracelet, but a little hurt that Joe would take it and hide it. She felt thankful she had happened onto his secret stash, but she wondered what other secrets he was keeping, probably even some he couldn't name. Her emotions folded on top of each other, getting bigger and thicker. It almost felt dangerous to hold so many intense emotions at once.

Julie emptied the crumbs of food from his pillowcase. She put the *Sorry!* piece in her pocket, put the bracelet on her wrist, and she moved the picture to his bedside table. She wouldn't take it away. She'd silently show him this was his to keep.

This whole family is his to keep.

Love is a decision.

Family is a decision.

A decision she could make, even on these days when she didn't feel it.

PART III

A few years later

Caroline, age 16

Joe, age 11

CHAPTER 14

The Strapsons had long stretches of time that were peaceful and normal. There were meals without arguments, days without fights, and weeks without trauma triggers. Sometimes it's hard to realize how wonderful normal can be, until normal is interrupted again.

Caroline and Joe were both growing up. Caroline was now in tenth grade, excelling in musical theater, and almost learning to drive. Joe was eleven, and he was bigger and stronger. His words were more intentional. He knew how to use them as weapons when he wanted to. The mostly joyful little boy had faded into a moody, almost-teenager. They all had to work harder to know him; to penetrate the wall he kept around his heart.

Joe was lying on his bottom bunk, earbuds in his ears and iPhone in his hand, when Caroline walked in.

"Hi, Joe."

He didn't respond.

She moved into his line of vision. "Hello, Joe."

He raised his eyebrows and then lowered them in half-greeting.

"Can I sit down?" she asked.

"Mm," he grunted.

She sat down next to his feet, his shoes on. She put her hand on his shoe and jiggled his foot.

"Joe."

He looked up, only his eyes moving to acknowledge her.

"I wanted to talk to you."

He didn't respond.

"I got you a present," she said.

He took out his earbuds. "What?"

"Ah, now he responds," she said, jiggling his shoe again.

"I'm listening," he put the phone face down on the bed but kept one earbud in. "What is it?"

She held out her palm, revealing two braided leather bracelets.

"What is it?" he asked again.

"I thought, maybe, I mean, it feels silly now, but it seemed like a good idea a few minutes ago… I thought maybe we could each wear these."

He raised his eyebrows again.

"You know, like a brother and sister, thing?"

His face showed no response.

"You could wear one, and I could wear one. I mean, they're kind of cool, right?"

Joe picked one up from the palm of her hand.

"Cool. Kind of." His eyes met hers.

"I thought maybe you could wear this."

He looked at the bracelet.

She spoke into the silence. "You're my brother."

After a few seconds, he said, "Okay."

"Okay, what?"

"Okay, everything. I'm your brother."

"So, you'll wear it?"

"Whatever. Yes."

Caroline smiled. "Yay! I'll put it on you."

He held out his wrist, and she tied the leather strands around his arm.

"Not too tight," he said.

"How's that?" she asked, reaching for the scissors on his desk.

"Fine. Good."

She trimmed the extra strands, securing the knot. "There. Can you tie mine on?"

He sat up and took the bracelet from her hand. He tied it around her wrist and trimmed the ends.

"No stupid names," Joe said.

"What do you mean?"

"'Bracelet buddies,' or whatever."

Caroline laughed. "Agreed. Just brother and sister."

Joe lay back on his pillow, and he put his earbuds back in, picking up his phone again.

She touched his shoe again. Then she got up and left him alone.

After she left the room, he touched the braided leather.

He decided in that moment, he'd wear it forever.

CHAPTER 15

"Where's my phone?" Joe said from the backseat. He was searching through his backpack, becoming more and more frantic and agitated. "Where's my phone? Who stole it?"

"Nobody stole your phone, Joe," Strapp said, looking at his son in the rearview mirror as he approached a stoplight. "I have it."

"Then you better give it back to me."

"You broke the rules, Joe. You know the consequences. Your phone is not a right, it's a—"

"Privilege. Shut up. I know already. This family is so jacked up!"

Joseph leaned forward to see Caroline finger scrolling through the music choices on her phone. "Why does she get hers?"

"Caroline? Because she didn't text her friends to buy drugs."

"Of course she didn't." Joe muttered something under his breath.

Strapp said, "Joe, if you have something to say, please say it."

"I said she's fucking perfect, you asshole."

Strapp's voice was stern. "Watch your language, son."

"Whatever. Of course. Take her side. Again."

The light turned green. Strapp turned onto the on-ramp, merging with traffic onto the highway.

Caroline looked at her brother and said, "Why are you always so mean to me? We're not on opposite teams, Joe. And I'm not perfect." She looked back at her phone.

Joe erupted with a guttural raging scream. He lunged toward Caroline, slapping the phone out of her hand. It slammed against the dashboard and then fell to the floor.

Caroline gasped. Her hands were open, shocked into stillness.

Strapp said, "Joseph! That is enough!"

"You better give me my phone back." Joe formed his hands into fists. Opening and closing his fists, over and over.

Though Strapp could only partially see Joe in the rearview mirror as he drove, he could sense that an explosion was nearing. Joe's rage had escalated to that point far too many times now. Sometimes Joe could take a deep breath and stay above his rage; other times he could lose all control. If only Strapp had pulled the car over moments ago when he had the chance. Now he was in heavy traffic on the interstate while an emotional timebomb was ticking in the backseat. Even the air in the car has shifted. Everything felt thick. Something was rising. A breaking point was near.

Strapp attempted to de-escalate the situation. He lowered his voice. "We can talk about this when we get home, Joe."

"NO. We can talk about it now. Give me my damn phone!"

Strapp saw an exit ahead. It wasn't the preferred way home, but he was certain they would not make it home before Joe's frayed nerves would break loose. Strapp turned on his blinker to get into the right lane when suddenly he felt a blow to the back of his head. Strapp's head bashed forward into the steering wheel.

"Oh my God! *Daddy!*" Caroline screamed. She pushed herself against the passenger window, screaming.

Strapp struggled to keep the car on the road as the fury of force from the backseat continued. It all happened so fast that Strapp had no idea what had just occurred. His vision was suddenly blurred. He could see taillights… hear horns honking, Caroline screaming, Joe raging.

Joe hit him again, now unloading his fury in repeated punches into the back of Strapp's head.

"Joe! Stop! *Stop!* STOP IT!" Caroline pleaded frantically.

Strapp grabbed for the steering wheel as the truck swerved onto the shoulder of the highway, and he jerked the wheel, pulling the truck back onto the road.

Joe leaned forward into the front seat, pinning Strapp to the driver's side window. He landed punch after punch into Strapp's head, back, and ribs. Strapp has his left hand on the wheel, and his right hand was extended toward Caroline, hoping to shield her.

At first Strapp could feel nothing. It was all terrifyingly sudden.

Then, just as suddenly, Strapp's mind began to slow down, as though everything had gone into slow motion. He could hear Caroline screaming and crying. He could sense the searing pain with each punch. He could hear the other cars honking and feel the truck accelerating as he tried to regain control.

Then everything stopped.

The punching, the honking, the crying, the screaming. Suddenly silence.

It was as if someone pushed the pause button on the scene. Only the traffic was still moving. Just as quickly as it had started, the unleashed horror of the moment stopped.

Strapp pulled to the shoulder of the exit ramp as traffic raced by. His hands were glued tightly to the steering wheel, his heart racing, his head dizzy.

Joe's rage had become a whimper. He sounds like a wounded animal in the backseat.

Caroline's eyes were wide with fear as she gasped for air. She had taken off her seat belt and had thrust herself up against the dashboard of the truck, nearly on the floorboard. She pulled her hands to her face and began to sob.

Strapp first leaned over to Caroline. He touched her arm gently. "Honey, are you okay? Did he hit you?"

"No," she gasped between ragged breaths. She lowered her hands to look at her dad. "He didn't hit me. Daddy…are you okay?"

"Yes. I will be fine."

"Dad, I'm scared."

"I know, baby. I'm here."

Strapped turned his eyes to the back seat. "Joe?"

Joe was curled into a ball on the floor in the backseat. He began to cry. "What did I do? I don't know what happened... I am sorry! *I am so sorry!* I don't know what is going on! What did I do? Oh my God.... What did I do? Why did I do that.... *oh my God...what did I do?"*

Joe began to wail. He made a fist again, but this time he bit the palm of his hand as he rocked back and forth.

"Get out of the car, Caroline," Strapp said firmly.

"Daddy—"

"Caroline. Open the door. Get out of the car."

With her eyes on her dad, she reached for the handle and opened the car door.

"I've got you, sweetheart. Step out of the car."

She sat frozen in place, with the passenger door open. Her eyes were wide. She was holding her breath.

"Caroline," Strapp said again, his voice even and firm.

But she had gone into shock.

Strapp opened his own door, stepped out and came to her side of the car. When Strapp reached her side, Caroline was still gazing out the driver's side window, where he had been.

He leaned into the car, holding her chin. He turned her face toward his. Her eyes were wide and dazed.

"Sweetheart, listen to Dad. I've got you. Come with me, Caroline. Get out of the car." He put a hand under her elbow, gently lifting her to her feet. Together they took a few faltering steps away from the road and into the grass. Strapp held his daughter's arm as she slowly sat down onto the grass.

He looked back to the car, then reached for the phone in his pocket. He dialed 9-1-1.

"What is your emergency?"

Strapp searched for the words. How could he find the words for what had just happened to his family?

"I...uh...my son has attacked me in my truck. I need help immediately. Please send someone." He disconnected the call, and then waited, trying to come to grips with this emergency.

Within minutes, two police cars arrived on the scene. Strapp sat with Caroline, his arm around her and rubbing her back, as they watched the officers take Joseph from the truck. The officers put handcuffs on Joe's wrists, and they placed him in the back of one of the officer's car.

Caroline couldn't bring herself to watch. She turned to Strapp and buried her face in his chest. She began to cry again as she finally found her voice. "Daddy...Daddy, I can't do this. I can't..."

Strapp held his daughter in his arms while he watched his son's profile in the officer's car.

"I'm sorry, baby. I'm sorry."

Sorry for so many things, he said to himself.

• • •

When they arrived at home, Julie was sitting at the dining room table, her laptop open. Caroline ran past her mom and up the stairs, skipping them two at a time.

"Hello, sweetheart... Caroline?"

Strapp walked into the dining room. Red scratches blazed on his neck and a large red welt was beginning to rise on his right cheek. Julie stood and came to his side without a word. Eyeing the welt, she gently touched it with her fingertips. "Strapp? Honey? What on earth... what happened? Where is Joseph?"

"Julie, please sit down."

Strapp relayed the events and the details he knew his wife would need to learn; the phone, the attack, the police, Caroline, and...Joe. They called Dex, Joe's therapist. They asked him to go to the police station and tend to their son while they tended to their daughter.

Everything felt broken.

So deeply broken.

CHAPTER 16

Strapp and Julie silently climbed the stairs to Caroline's bedroom.

Caroline was lying on her bed, facing the window. Julie sat down behind her, rubbing her back. Strapp sat down on the chair by the window, facing his daughter. No one said anything for a few minutes.

Finally, Strapp moved closer to Caroline, gently stroking her hair. "I love you, Caroline."

"He's getting bigger, Daddy. Stronger. Smarter. His words hurt a lot more—he knows what he's saying now."

"You are right, honey," he said gently. "I am so sorry about what happened today."

"It's not your fault, Dad." Caroline rolled over onto her back so she could see her mother, too. "It's not yours either."

"And it's not yours either," Julie said.

"Caroline, your mother and I have made some decisions. We are intent upon doing everything we can to keep our family safe, and that looks different for you and for Joe. Your safety calls for different decisions. We've decided he's not coming home tonight, Caroline."

She sat up in bed. "I don't want him to leave, though."

"It's not forever; it's just until we know the next plan."

"Where will he go?"

"When he leaves the police station, he will go to the hospital for the night, and he will stay there until there is a bed at a group home where he can get the help he needs."

"But how will we help him?" Caroline asked. "We can't give up on him."

"We aren't giving up on him," Julie said. "But this is no longer a safe place for him to be. And we can care for him and help him, even if he doesn't live with us."

"Can we see him?" she asked.

"Do you want to?" Julie asked.

"I…. I don't know," Caroline said, putting her forearm over her eyes.

"You don't have to know, Caroline," Julie said, taking her daughter's hand. "It's all a shock. Of course you don't know."

Caroline looked up at the ceiling. "It's hard enough when he hurts me. But to watch him hurt you guys? To see him beat up my dad today?" A tear fell from the corner of her eye, rolling down to her ear lobe. "Why does this have to be so hard? Why can't he just receive what he has been given?"

"Honey, I think he wants to," Strapp said gently. "He just doesn't know how."

"Then let's teach him."

Julie smiles. "Caroline, tell me what you know about the day you were born."

"Well...I don't exactly remember it, Mom."

"But you've heard us talk about it. What do you know? How did we feel, as your mom and dad?" Julie asks.

"I guess...I think you were happy."

"Sweetheart, we were over the moon. We were so happy you were born, and you were ours. Our very own baby girl! We used to argue over who got to go into your nursery when you woke up from your nap. Honestly, most of the time we held you even while you slept. We loved those moments of holding you, kissing you, singing to you, and learning all about you. Remember that, Strapp?"

"I'll never forget it," Strapp smiled.

"And when you cried, we wanted to know why. Is she hungry? Is she wet? What does she need? Anytime you made a sound, we jumped at the chance to help you, to meet your needs."

Caroline listened silently.

"Honey, nobody did that for Joe. No one cared for him in kind ways when he was a baby, and they didn't meet his needs when he began to grow. A baby truly needs someone to hear them, touch them, and hold them."

"And his parents didn't do that?"

"We don't know their whole story, honey, but...no. Joe didn't get the loving care he needed when he was small, and it created a wound in his brain," Julie explained. "When babies get the love they need, their brains learn how to attach to someone. They learn how to trust. Joseph had no one to answer his cries, to teach him how to trust and feel loved."

"Nobody?"

"Not until he got here. He's learning things for the first time in our home, and there's no place for his brain to hold this kind of love."

"But that's not his life, now. It's different here," Caroline says. "He has a mom and a dad who love him. He has a bedroom and a bed and a house and… stuff. He has me."

"And he has no real understanding of how to receive any of those things," Julie says. "So, he pushes us away."

Caroline looks at her dad, the marks on his face and neck, the swelling at his cheekbone. "Or punches you."

"Yes," Strapp says. "And even though that's what makes sense to him, it's not okay in our home. We will keep you safe, Caroline."

She sits up in her bed, looking back and forth between her parents. "I don't know what to do."

"We will help you," Strapp said, rubbing her knee.

"We will keep you safe," Julie says, stroking Caroline's hair, sweeping it behind her ear. "Honey, it's important for you to know that you don't have to be his mom. That's my job. There are things we must do to help Joe because we are his parents. But you don't have to be his mom."

"I just want to be his sister. What does a sister do when her brother is dangerous? What do I do when I don't want to be near him?"

“You can love him from where you are. And that doesn’t have to be right beside him,” Strapp said. “We are choosing to forgive him, honey. We want to keep showing him how to live in a family, but forgiving him doesn’t mean we let him hurt you, babe. We will keep you safe.”

“Safe,” Caroline repeated the word. “I don’t feel like I know what that means anymore.”

CHAPTER 17

"What's on your mind today, Strapp?" The two men sat facing each other at a picnic table in the park. Strapp's notebook lay on the table, always at the ready. It seemed that anytime Hank spoke, Strapp wanted to write it down.

Strapp exhaled. He leaned forward, rests his elbows on his knees.

"Things are beginning to change. But not in a good way."

"What's going on, Strapp?"

"Hank, we may need to send Joseph to a wilderness therapy program. I think he needs more help than we can give him."

"Tell me about the program," Hank said.

"It's apparently a treatment program that takes teenagers out of their familiar environments so that the therapists can reach the kids in their pain. Joe would spend two or three months in a wilderness setting, receiving nonstop therapy."

"How does that make you feel as you think of sending your son away?"

Tears burned Strapp's eyes.

"I feel horrible, but I don't know what else we can do. Things are so out of control. He's bigger now, Hank. He has grown tall, and strong. What were once angry verbal outbursts have now grown into physical outbursts. He punches the wall, he throws things… he has lost control, and I feel like we have, too. It's getting worse—he's nearly as strong as I am now."

"He's not a little boy anymore, Strapp."

"No, sir. And that little boy that Julie could hold in her arms? His strength far outweighs hers now. She's afraid of what might happen—we both are. And we feel hopeless. Julie and I feel like we have let him down. I'm crushed, Hank."

They sat in silence for a moment.

Finally, Hank spoke. "Can I tell you what I see?"

"Yes. Yes, please."

Hank's voice was gentle. "I see a father and a mother that love their son deeply. I see a set of parents who are doing everything in their power to help their son find peace in his life."

"That's all I want for him."

"But there is a war waging inside your son. The orphan spirit is not going to go down easy, that is all he knows at this point. But that is what is so powerful about the love of a father and a mother. Right now, you and Julie want more for Joe than he wants for himself. He can't see it right now, but you are stepping in to be a peacemaker in his life. You are showing him mercy."

"Mercy?" Strapp asked.

"Open your notebook, son. *Mercy* means putting yourself into the skin of another person, so you begin to see, feel, and hear what they do."

Strapp wrote it down. *Mercy. Feel what he feels.*

"That's just it, Hank," Strapp said. "I am having a hard time understanding my son. I try to put myself in his skin, but it is impossible for me to feel the things he feels. I don't understand the rejection that he has experienced in his life, and I cannot change his story or erase the hurt he feels. But we offer something so much better. Why won't he simply receive what we want to give him?"

"Strapp, your son is still trying to learn this very important trait of sonship. An orphan is only concerned with self. They can't see past their own problems, their unmet deep needs. Until he receives the mercy that his Father in Heaven has for him, he will never be able to truly have mercy for others."

"It isn't just my son who is learning, Hank. I don't think I fully understand mercy."

"Well, I'll tell you this: in order to give mercy, we must learn to receive it. Very similar to loving our neighbors, we need to first learn to love ourselves. Mercy is the same flow. We must receive it to give it."

Strapp wrote it down. *Receive mercy, then give it.*

He said, "We can't offer Joe everything that this world offers, but we can certainly give him opportunities. We can offer him things that he has never dreamed of or imagined. We love him so much, but he won't receive it and I find myself getting angry. I find myself mad at him for not accepting what we want to give to him freely!"

Hank took a deep breath, allowing Strapp to hang on to the last words that came from his mouth.

"That's an interesting emotion," Hank responded.

"Which emotion? I'm feeling a lot of them right now."

"Anger...why are you mad at your son for not being willing to receive what you want to freely give to him?" Hank paused to let his words sink in. "Who is this about, Strapp? Is this about Joseph? Or is this about *you*?"

Strapp seemed to cave under the weight of the conviction in the question. His shoulders bowed. "Am I the orphan, Hank?"

Hank put his hand on Strapp's shoulder. "We all are son. We all have this war raging inside us, this inability to receive what God is offering. We all think like orphans, when really, we are children of God. While we were still sinners, Christ died for us. In other words, while the war was raging within us, the war for our soul, God sent his son to die for all of mankind. Can you imagine that, Strapp?"

"I'm not sure I can."

Hank continued. "Mercy involves getting inside the skin of another person, feeling what they feel. This is exactly what God did when he sent his son. Jesus took the flesh of a man, in order to experience everything we have experienced, including the temptations, the fears, the pain. He was mercy in the flesh. Strapp, God knew that there was only one way that you could once again be in relationship with him. He had to send his son to come to this world to be crucified, knowing that there was no assurance that you would in turn choose him to be your Father. God took the first step in making peace with you."

They sat in silence for a minute, before Hank spoke again. "Strapp, can I ask you a very difficult question?"

Strapp laughed under his breath. "Something tells me I don't have a choice, so fire away."

"How much do you love your son?"

Strapp looked up. He met Hank's eyes. "More than you know, Hank."

"Do you love him enough that you would sacrifice Caroline in order to adopt him, knowing that he may never choose you?"

Strapp's jaw tightened. He shook his head. "I can't…I can't answer that question."

"It's an impossible question, I know. Your son told you he hates you. Do you suppose God has ever heard those words?"

"From his son? Do you mean Jesus? I don't think Jesus said that to him, no."

"Jesus was his son, yes, and so are you. Every single person is invited to become his son or daughter. We start as orphans, and when we choose a relationship with God, we become his sons and daughters. By adoption, actually."

Strapp folded his hands again. He shook his head. "You're kind of blowing my mind a little bit."

"Stay with me here. Let's just think about it: do you suppose God has felt this way? Rejected by a child he loves?"

"Yes, when you put it that way. Especially the ones who don't want a relationship with him at all. The ones who refuse 'adoption,' as you said it." Strapp gestured with air quotes.

"So, the parallels are many, Strapp. You wanted Joe, you chose him, you prepared a place for him. You want to give that child your name, your protection, your resources, your strength, your wisdom, your inheritance—"

"Yes. I want to give him every single bit of the safety and security and identity that comes with being in our family. Everything I have given to Caroline, I want it for Joe, too."

"But he's saying he doesn't want it."

Strapp's eyes filled with tears. "And it's killing me."

Hank raised his eyebrows, letting the words linger in the air. Then he said, "It killed Jesus, too."

PART IV

Joe, age 15

Caroline, age 19

CHAPTER 18

College was certainly the natural next stage in life for Caroline, and it was time for her to go. But when she moved out of their home, her absence triggered all of Joe's old abandonment wounds. He had regressed in many ways, and his choices were not only dangerous, but often illegal.

A spot opened for Joe in a juvenile residential treatment facility, and the Strapsons were hopeful that this would be a safe step for Joe. They hoped that a place with specialists and devoted staff would be a safer option, but Joe had a different plan. On the third day, Joseph decided that he had had enough of his new residential placement. He carried his backpack to load the van along with the other residents on their way to his new school, but instead of climbing aboard, Joe took off.

He had run away before, and a typical escape lasted an hour or two. His escapes never seemed to be premeditated; he was usually triggered by some wave of fear, anxiety, or anger, and he'd split. Joe would be gone for a little while, and they always found him at a nearby McDonald's where he had gone to grab a quick burger, a milkshake, a cigarette, and a few minutes to calm down.

This time, he had gone missing for two hours, and then he had shown up on the back porch of their home. He had taken an Uber to their house, and they found him reclining in a deck chair, his feet up on the table, a cigarette in his hand. Joe had looked at them like this was no big deal, as if it were no surprise that he would come for a visit, no surprise that he would show up on their property when nearly every officer in the whole city was looking for him.

They had taken him back to the residential facility, and they had gone through the standard protocol for intake of a patient. They opened his duffel bag to check his belongings for contraband. They expected to find the cigarettes he loved but was not allowed to bring with him. Instead, they were surprised to find a cigar, two gold necklaces, and $200 in cash.

The cigar and cash were stolen from Strapp's humidor in his office.

The necklaces were stolen from Julie's jewelry box in her closet.

Joseph had come home just long enough to smoke and to steal from them.

Just long enough to break their hearts in a brand-new way.

Strapp and Julie were unspeakably exhausted.

• • •

Joe didn't live with them anymore, and they only saw him when they visited him at the residential facility, or on days like this—in family therapy. Strapp and Julie sat across from him on a couch in the therapist's office. Dex sat in his chair in the corner of the space, a neutral place of mediation. Very gifted at what he does as a therapist,

Dex is young, half Asian, very educated not only in the books, but also in life. He had a rough childhood as well, but he was able to navigate his way through it and eventually found his calling as a therapist for troubled youth. He talks like the kids, in their lingo, and in their language.

They had been seeing Dex for nearly a year, and he had guided their family through this season of turmoil. When Joe was arrested for shoplifting, Dex had attended his hearing in the courtroom, and he stood as a witness on the stand confirming his home life and family support. When Joe ran away from home, Dex had joined the search to find Joe and bring him back to safety. In the darkest moments, when Joe was contemplating taking his own life, Dex was one of the first people he would call. Dex had shepherded them through their struggles.

There were times that Joseph acted like he didn't want to talk with Dex, but that was typically because he could feel himself starting to draw closer to him. Dex had helped them all to see that this pattern is a symptom of Reactive Attachment Disorder, one of several formal diagnoses that Joseph had received.

Today, Julie and Strapp sat with their son in Dex's office.

"I don't know why we even have to do this," Joe said. He was fifteen years old now, slouched low in the middle of a loveseat in the therapist's office. Joe tugged on the t-shirt sleeve of his left arm, inspecting and scratching a small scab on his new tattoo.

"Sweetheart," Julie began, her voice even, "we just want to talk to you."

"Well, I don't want to talk to you."

"I understand that, but we're trying to do what is best for you—"

"I. Don't. Want. It."

"Joe—" Strapp began to speak, but Dex interrupted him.

"Strapp, Julie, let's give Joe a chance to speak first. Joe, would you like to share with your parents what we discussed yesterday?"

"Not really. What does it matter anyway?"

Dex took off his glasses and set them on the table beside him. "Well, it matters because *you* matter."

"I don't want to be here. I don't want to do family therapy anymore. I told you that," he looked again at his tattoo, scratching and inspecting. "I don't know why we have to keep doing this; coming to this stupid office, talking about everything that's already happened. It happened and I am sorry, but it is what it is and there is nothing I can do about it now."

"I understand that you feel that way, Joe," Dex's voice was always even and intentional. "But communication is part of being in a family. That means each person gets to talk, and it also means each person needs to listen. Would you like to talk first? Or listen?"

"You want to know what else pisses me off? There is no purpose to these meetings! What's the goal? All you want to do is come in here and ask ME a bunch of questions to find out why I do the things I do. We don't need a family therapy session to do that! Just ask me and I will tell you." He folded his arms and stared at the floor. "You know what? Screw it…I have nothing to say."

"Then we'll let your parents speak, and you get to listen now. Strapp? What would you like to say to Joe?"

Strapp leaned forward and rested his elbows on his knees, leaning as close to his son as he could. "Joe, I am a little confused right now. I hear you say that all we have to do is ask you why you do things and you will tell us. But there have been many times after you have done something wrong that you have called me crying, saying that you have no idea why you did what you did."

"Well, sometimes I don't know why."

"And that is why this time is so important. I want to be honest with you about a few things, okay?'

"Whatever."

Dex interrupted. "Joe, look at me, please."

Joe tightened his jaw but lifted his eyes to look at Dex.

"Hey, bud?" Dex said, "They're trying. Please don't be a dick right now."

Dex dropped cuss words often into his conversations with Joe. It's uncomfortable for Strapp and Julie, but they have learned that his word choices are intentional. He affirms Joseph's feelings in words that he can relate to. It is a powerful tool that was hard for Strapp and Julie to adjust to, but they are seeing progress in their sessions.

Sure enough, Joe looks at his dad.

"I don't want to speak for your mom, but I am going to tell you why I want to come to these family sessions. Pal, I am not interested in rehashing your mistakes of the past. I really don't enjoy that."

"And yet, here we are." Joe rolled his eyes.

Dex interrupted, "Joe, your job right now is to *listen.* Strapp, please continue."

"Joe, I'm not trying to change who you are, and we're not trying to make you do something you don't want to do. I'm here because I want to be in relationship with my son. Not only for the next few years, but for the rest of my life. Yes, I am your father, but I want to be your dad."

Joe scoffed. "Is there a difference?"

"There is, Joe. The judge in the courtroom declared that I'm your father. The law formed that relationship, but it's the bond between your heart and mine that takes us to a new level. That's what makes me your dad. Thirty years from now, when I'm seventy years old and you're forty, I want to still have a relationship with you. I want to still be your dad then."

"You'll be old."

"That's true," Strapp nodded. "But I will still love you, and I will still want everything that's best for you. I'm sitting here today, staying in these hard conversations with you, all so we can still be in relationship then."

Joe looked at the floor.

Dex said, "Joe what do you think about what your Dad just said?"

"I have worked my ass off in school. My grades were improving. And some smart-ass punk says something to me, *he* starts the fight, and then—BAM. One stupid mistake and it all goes away. What's the purpose of working so hard when I know I am going to fail and lose it all anyway? I know you are disappointed in me, and I'm sick of feeling that on my shoulders. I can't take it."

Dex sits up in his chair, "Joseph, let's talk more about that incident that happened at school."

"Which one?"

"The one you just mentioned. With the dude in the classroom."

"I punched him in the face. He had it coming."

"Why did he have it coming?"

"He was talking shit about my dudes," Joe said. "I had to man up."

"Man up? So, you hit him?"

"I told you, he had it coming."

"Let me ask you, Joe. Who won that fight?"

"I did."

"You think so? Because the way I see it," Dex said, "You're the one looking at assault charges and a day in court. That dude is free."

"That's because this is all some jacked up shit."

"No, Joe, it's because being a man means practicing restraint. It means not flying off the handle every time you're mad."

Joe looked at the floor. "You don't understand."

"I know you feel that way, Joe, but I am trying to understand. We all are. We're trying to help you to live in the moment you're in; to become a young man who can take responsibility for his words and his actions."

"I can't change what I did."

"But…?" Dex held out his hands. He and Joe had gone over this many times. He waited for him to add the second half of that thought.

Joe said, "I know, I know. I can't change the past, but I can certainly change my future by remaining in the present. You have told me that a thousand times!"

"There it is!" Dex said, raising a closed fist to bump knuckles with Joe. "Nice job, my brotha! This family therapy thing really does work—don't ya think?"

"Yeah, yeah, yeah," Joe lazily raised his knuckles to meet Dex's.

"Okay, then it's your mom's turn. Julie?"

Julie uncrossed her legs and leaned forward and took Joseph's hand. "Joe, sweetheart, I'm not here to rehash everything that's already happened. You're right, honey. We can't change those things."

"That's what I freaking said already."

"Joe," Dex was always so consistent. "It's not your turn. Julie, please continue."

"We can't fix what has been done, but we *can* create new. We can start something new together—all of us—anytime you want to. We can begin today, moving forward in a healthy way."

Joe stared at the floor.

Julie saw the white board on the wall in Dex's office, and she got an idea. She walked over to the board and drew a dotted line across the middle. On the left side of the board, far above the dotted line, she drew a dot. She said, "Joseph, please look at this."

He looked up at the board.

Julie said, "This dotted line, Joe, is the line of trust. Let's imagine that's where trust lives, and we want to stay far above that line to have trust in each other. This dot, way up here? That's where we started when you first came home, so many years ago. We always start with trust."

She drew a dot a bit lower and to the right. She connected them. "And then maybe you would tell me a little lie, just something small. And my trust in you drops a bit."

She drew another dot to the right, a little higher than the second, but not as high as the first one. "And then you would apologize, you'd make some good and honest choices, and you'd build a little of that trust back."

She drew a lower dot. "And then you punch someone."

She drew a lower dot. "And then you steal something from our home."

She drew a lower dot. "And then I learn that you've been doing drugs."

She drew another dot, a little higher. "And then we get a little upturn when I see you here because you show up for counseling."

She drew a lower dot, below the dotted line. "And then you run away from your facility."

She connected the dots with a jagged line. "Joe, do you see that it looks like a heartbeat? It goes up and down, up and down, up and down. And we need to keep it above this dotted line. Because that's where trust lives."

She came back and sat down. She took her son's hand. "Joseph, sweetheart," Julie's voice was low and tender, "We're not going to leave you. But we need to rebuild some trust."

Joe kept his eyes on the floor. "I can't seem to shake you guys, no matter what I do."

Julie exhaled. "That's what I want you to know, more than anything."

Joe's jaw tightened. "I hear you. I get it."

Then Joe lifted his eyes to meet Strapp's eyes. Joe said, "But that doesn't mean I won't leave you."

CHAPTER 19

Strapp parked his truck at the end of a dirt road, far out in the wilderness. Hank was leading him on another discovery trip.

Strapp had come to love his time with Hank. Their friendship was growing deeper, and their love for one another was obvious to everyone. As the dust settled around the truck, Strapp was the first to get out of the truck and stand on the edge of a beautiful cliff, overlooking the valley below. Hank joined his friend and they stood in silence, taking in the sounds of nature.

Strapp took in a deep breath, and he let it out in a long exhale.

"Strapp, you had an earthly father who modeled presence and unconditional love. So, it's perhaps easy for you to view God as a loving Father. But Joe didn't have that dad before you. He has no idea what to do with this kind of unconditional love, this pursuit of relationship."

Strapp paused to think, then said, "Hank, let me ask you, what happens when expectations don't meet reality?"

"That's a big question, Strapp."

"It's the biggest one I'm wrestling with right now. I'm trying to figure it all out. This place where we've landed with Joseph... lay it on me, Hank. I have to know. Do you think this is a reflection on me?"

"A reflection on you?" Hank asked.

"Have I done something wrong? Did I mess something up? I mean, did Julie and I misunderstand God and what He wanted us to do? I am starting to feel like everything I believed about God isn't true."

Hank asked, "Well, let me ask you this. When someone rejects God, does that mean God is a bad father?"

"I would never say that."

"I don't think anybody would say that, Strapp. The truth is, he's a perfect parent, and even his kids reject him. Think about it—even Adam and Eve disobeyed and rejected him, without the cultural influences we have today. They had one thing that was off limits, and they were drawn to it. Even with the pure love of God, so tangible in their lives, they rejected it. Do you think God did something wrong?"

Strapp paused, letting the concept sink into his mind and heart. "I had never thought of it that way."

"So why does your heart go there first? Why do you assume you're a bad father if your son is rejecting you? Strapp, I'll tell you this: there comes a point for every parent—whether you've adopted or created the child you're raising—where you have to evaluate yourself and decide if there are ways to parent better than you've been parenting. These are good and healthy questions for any parent to ask and consider."

"It seems like it all boils down to that. I think my parenting is the daily journey of asking that question."

"I agree, Strapp. And so, to answer your question, I would say, it's okay."

"What do you mean, 'it's okay?'"

"Strapp, you've done all that you've known to do. Sure, you and Julie are not perfect parents, but you've done what you knew how to do, right?"

"That's all we've ever done. We made the best decision with the information and resources we had."

"Would you and Julie take credit for the incredible young lady Caroline has become?"

Strapp laughed. "No way. She was *born* amazing. We can't take credit for that."

"And yet, you seem more than willing to take the responsibility for Joe's poor decisions. You seem to be taking the blame for his choice to disobey, and he has chosen not to love you back. Strapp, I'd venture to say most of the parents I know take too much credit if it goes well, and they take too much blame if it goes wrong."

Strapp was silent.

Hank said, "What if I told you that you won't be judged on Joe's decisions?"

Strapp said, "I've never considered that possibility. Everything about the world seems formulaic, and the church has always seemed to tell me that there's a blessing formula. Me, plus my obedience, plus God, equals blessing."

"That sounds very transactional, Strapp."

"Well, we live in a transactional world, Hank."

"Hmmm. So, you're telling me that if you're an obedient parent, following all the rules, and if God is the faithful God he claims to be, then the result should be this great young man who is training to be the next Billy Graham, or the President of the United States—"

"Or maybe, at least just a kind person to other human beings," Strapp interrupted.

"And that's not what happened."

"Not at all. That's not *at all* what happened."

"Then you have to go back to the formula and change something. Either God is not pulling his weight, or somehow you've failed."

"Which brings me back to my initial question, Hank. Basically, I've concluded that either I'm a loser, or God is not good. Maybe he doesn't exist. Maybe I'm a failure, or maybe he has failed me."

"Or you've tried to put God into a formula he never created."

"A possibility, I suppose."

"Strapp, follow me—there is something I want to show you."

Hank stood to his feet and started walking down a nearby trail. Strapp reluctantly followed, wondering where Hank may be leading him.

"Where are we going?"

"Come on, big fella. I think you will want to see this. Just stay close, I don't want you to get lost." Hank replied with a smile and a wink.

Hank and Strapp follow the trail down a winding path and into a valley. Hank turns and looks at Strapp. "Now what do you see?"

Strapp looked up at the hills, trees, and sky around him. "I see a whole lot of beauty."

"Look down, too."

Strapp obeyed, looking down at the cluster of wildflowers around his feet. He knelt and touched the delicate white petals of a bell-shaped flower. "Those are some of the whitest flowers I have ever seen. I mean, those flowers are over-the-top white. What are they called?"

"These are called Lilies of the Valley."

"Aren't those mentioned in the Bible?" Strapp asked.

"They are, yes. They're mentioned as flowers, but the Lily of the Valley is also a name for God. He is described as the Lily of the Valley."

"I wouldn't have drawn the parallel between a delicate flower and the Maker of the Universe."

"What's amazing, Strapp, is that you can't see these tiny, beautiful flowers from the mountaintop. You can only find them in the valley. And in the same way, there are some characteristics of the heart of God that we can only experience in the valleys of life. In the difficult moments that He allows, we can experience a whole new depth of his presence."

Strapp rose to stand again beside Hank.

Hank said, "Brother, it sounds to me like you've found yourself in the valley."

Strapp slid his hands into the pockets of his jeans. "You could say that."

"But Strapp, if you're looking for him, you'll find him in this valley in a unique way. You'll find him in ways he can't be found anywhere else."

"So, he lets these things happen, these disappointments and sufferings and losses, so we can see that he's here too."

"Yes, Strapp. He's the lily."

Hank let the silence linger. Then he said, "Strapp, it's clear that your expectations haven't aligned. This is not how you thought this would go. So, this is where the rubber meets the road… Do you trust him enough to say this is okay?"

Strapp exhaled a long, low breath. "I want to trust him that way. But I don't know if I do."

"That's a start, Strapp. He can work with that kind of honesty." Hank put a hand on his shoulder. "Strapp, hear me on this. At the end of the day, Joe must choose. You can't choose for him, and his choice will not be about you, a reflection on you, or a judgment of your parenting. The choice will simply be *his.*"

"The whole thing is shifting, Hank," Strapp said, "I thought I was supposed to learn about being a son, and I learned that there's so much I don't know. But now it seems that I'm learning about being a father, and I know even less, if that's possible."

"Say more about that, Strapp."

"It's easy to be a father when your kids are doing things that make you proud. Things that honor you as a parent. Like, when they are obedient, you know? It propagates this father-son relationship the way it's supposed to be. But that's not how it is with Joe. He doesn't want to obey; he doesn't want a relationship—he doesn't even want to have a conversation."

Tears began pooling in Strapp's eyes. "Hank, I don't know what to do! We are poured out. We have done everything we know to do, and nothing is working. My heart is broken. Julie and I feel like we are running out of time, like we are in a race against something we can't see, and we are starting to get scared. What are we supposed to do now?"

Hank nods toward the lilies. "That sounds like something you need to talk to Him about…"

Strapp dropped to his knees as his tears began to fall.

"Father, I really don't even know what to say, but I believe you are here. I know you are listening right now. At this point, I feel so hopeless…and for too long, I have allowed my identity to be wrapped up in the success or failures of my kids. Now I see how wrong I have been."

He paused to breathe, to think, and finally spoke again.

"You are such a good Dad to me. You have been patient with me, and you have shown me grace and mercy during the times that I didn't act much like a son. But you have also celebrated with me when I walked in obedience. No matter what, you have always been the same. You have always been a good Dad."

Strapp opened his hands to the sky, a gesture to both give and receive.

"God, you are a holy Father, a righteous judge, and a generous provider. Thank you for bringing Joe to our family. You have entrusted Julie and me with this young man. You have asked us to love him, protect him, and care for him as we do for our biological child. God, you and I both know that we have been far from perfect parents, but I pray that in our better days, we have reflected you and your love."

He took in another deep inhale and exhale, and then he said, "God, today, I give my son Joseph back to you. I know the choice is his. I ask Your Spirit to move in such a way that he can begin to see you in the same way that I have come to know you. He is yours."

CHAPTER 20

Joe was missing again, but this time it was different. He had executed a plan. He had packed a bag, physically assaulted three staff who stood in his way, and now he had been missing for six hours. It had been a long day and a long night.

Frankly, it had become a long few years.

Strapp and Julie lay awake in their bed. Strapp stared at the ceiling, his hands folded behind his head. Julie leaned back on pillows against the headboard, holding her phone in her hand, staring at the screen.

"I wish he would call us," Julie said.

Strapp reached over to take her hand. "I know, babe. Me too."

"Where do you think he is? I mean, where could he have gone? Do you think he's hungry? Is he safe?" She began to cry.

"Come here, babe," he said, pulling her toward him. She leaned into him and rested her head on his chest. He wrapped his arm around her, holding her close to him. He had no answers, and he didn't offer any.

"Strapp, did we make a mistake?" she said, so quietly he could barely hear her. "Should we have let him come back home?"

He looked up to the ceiling, and he stroked her hair. There isn't a manual for something like this, an instruction guide for the levels of guilt, anger, and sadness coursing through him. There isn't a map for 'how to love your kid who doesn't love you back.' He didn't know how to be the father his son needed. He only knew that he still loved his son.

"Sweetheart, when he is ready to come home, we will bring him home."

They waited through the night for a call. Hour after hour passed. They fell asleep holding their silent phones and each other.

• • •

The sun had not come up when his phone rang. Julie startled awake, bolting upright. She reached for her phone, and Strapp reached for her hand. "It's mine, babe. I got it."

He answered the call. "Hello?"

"Hello, Mr. Strapson?"

"Yes?"

"Mr. Strapson, this is detective Steve Johnson with the Sheriff's office. Is your son Joseph Strapson?"

"Yes, he is."

"Well sir, we have found your son."

Strapp exhaled, nodding to Julie. She clasped her hands together to her chest. "Oh, thank you, God," she said. Then she said, "Is he alive? Is he safe?"

Strapp took her hand again and said into the phone, "Where is he, officer?"

"We have him here in our custody at the public library. We will be transporting him to the Juvenile Assessment Center in the morning, where he will be processed into that facility. We wanted you to be aware that we have him, and he is safe."

"He is safe," he repeated the officer's words, putting his arm around Julie. "Can we come to the station to see him?"

"One moment, Mr. Strapson—"

Strapp heard a muffled conversation on the other end of the line, and then the officer said, "Mr. Strapson, your son has asked for no visitors tonight, and we suggest you do not come. You can visit him tomorrow morning during visiting hours at the Juvenile Center, and you can contact them directly for those times. Do you have any other questions?"

"Yes, sir. Did he say why he ran?"

"No, Mr. Strapson, he did not say."

"Okay. Thank you for your call, officer."

"Have a safe evening, Mr. Strapson."

And with a click, the line went silent.

Your son has asked for no visitors. We suggest you do not come. Those words hung in Strapp's mind as he set down his phone.

Julie immediately began questioning him. "So? What did they say?"

Strapp stared straight ahead. "They found him. He was at the Lakewood Public Library."

"The library? Why was he there? Is he okay? Did he have anything to eat?"

"Honey, I don't know. That is all they said."

"You spoke to them longer than that, Strapp. Where is he now? Where are they taking…." Julie paused. "I'm sorry, babe. Please… just tell me everything they said. I'll get dressed so we can leave right away to see him."

Strapp was still dazed by the call and staring into space. "They said that he doesn't want to see us."

"What? What do you mean, he doesn't want to see us?"

"They said they will take him to the juvenile detention center in the morning, and Joe doesn't want us to come visit him before then."

Julie's shoulders sank. Her face fell. "Why would he say that?"

"Babe, I don't know," Strapp said.

Then, suddenly the tone of his voice shifted. "You know, actually, at this point, I don't care what he wants. Get dressed, sweetheart. We are going to see our son."

CHAPTER 21

Strapp and Julie drove to the Juvenile Detention Facility, calling on their way. They intended to be there when he arrived, to see him as soon as they were allowed. An officer had taken their phone call and scheduled their visit. Strapp and Julie waited in the parking lot for the sun to come up and for the doors to open.

They arrived at the facility with only their driver's licenses, and they signed several pages of paperwork at the front desk. A disinterested officer pointed to a large metal door. "Visiting area is through that door. Please wait for the buzzer, and then go to room three."

Julie jumped when the buzzer sounded. Strapp reached for the large handle and pulled open the heavy metal door. They stepped into a stark and sterile room with doors on each wall. As instructed, they stood in front of door number 3, and Strapp reached for the handle of the door. It was locked.

Suddenly, another buzzer sounded, startling them both this time. He reached again for the handle, and the door opened to a small room with three chairs, a small wooden table, and another locked door. No pictures, no decorations. It was cold, bright, institutional, and uninviting. There were two security cameras mounted in the corner, and there was a small button on the wall with a red sign that read, "Assistance."

As they walked into the room, the door closed behind them, locking with a loud click. Everything got real.

Julie whispered, "What do we do?"

Strapp pulled the chair so it was next to the one he would sit in, and he gestured for her to sit down. "I think we just wait."

As they sat in the chairs, they could hear echoes of doors slamming outside their small room. They heard distant chatter, a shout, and then quiet again. Then they heard a series of doors unlocking, opening, and then closing again. They heard footsteps coming near, and then a new officer's face appeared in the window. He unlocked the door, leaned in, and said, "Mr. and Mrs. Strapson?"

"Yes, sir," Strapp answered.

The guard opened the door wider, letting Joseph come inside. He was wearing jail-issued khaki pants, a standard black shirt, and a pair of beige Crocs. He had shackles on his wrists and ankles. As Joe looked at the floor and the officer took off his handcuffs, Strapp noticed that his son's hair looked surprisingly clean.

"You have thirty minutes," the guard barked. He closed the door, and they heard the door click, locking them inside together.

Joseph was the first to break the silence. "I thought I told you not to come. Why in the hell are you here?"

"We wanted to see you," Julie replied.

"I said *no,*" Joe said, his voice shaking.

"Joe, why do you think we wouldn't want to come and see you?" Strapp added.

He looked at the floor. "It's not that. I just didn't want you to see me here."

Joseph began to cry.

Strapp reached across the table. He wanted to be closer to Joe, but he didn't want to cross his son's boundary. "I know, buddy. None of us ever thought it would ever come to this. and we certainly never thought we would ever be visiting you in a place like this. I understand that it is hard."

Joe made a fist and pounded the table. "No, you *don't* understand! You have no idea how hard it is to be in this place. I am not safe here. Do you understand me? *I am not safe!*"

Julie reached for him, but Joe jerked away from her reach. "No! Don't touch me. Let me tell you what it's like here. I can't sleep. I can't eat. The other kids take my food away from me. There is nothing I can do. Dad, do you realize that there are gangs in this place? They have put me in this pod where I am one of only two white kids, and they will beat the shit out of me. And guess whose fault it will be if they do? Yours—" he pointed at Strapp. "It will be *your fault.* That's who."

"Son," Strapp began.

"Don't call me that," Joe said. "If you would bail me out, then this would be over."

Strapp asked, "Do you want to come home, Joe?"

"No."

"Then I'm not here to talk you into coming home. If that's not the best place for you, then it's not what I want for you. You might not ever choose to move into our home again, and if that's what you choose, I will support that. My goal today is not to bring you home."

Joseph didn't respond, but he slowly looked up from the floor. Strapp has his undivided attention.

Silence hung in the air.

"I am just so tired of screwing up," Joe continued. "There is no use in trying anymore. Every time that I try hard to do the right thing, I eventually screw it up, and then I have to start all over again. It isn't worth it. I am tired of hurting everyone else with my actions. I give up."

He put his head in his hands, and he wept silently.

Julie and Strapp looked at each other. Julie's eyes were pleading to Strapp: "Do something, please do something."

Strapp put his hand on Joe's arm, and to his surprise, this time Joe didn't pull away.

"Son," he said, "You are right about one thing: it is very hard for your Mom and me to see you in this place. But please hear me, Joseph. No matter what happens to you, no matter what choices you make, no matter where you find yourself, we will always be here for you. We aren't giving up on you."

"Joe, we love you very much, honey," Julie said gently. "We just want to see you get the help you need so you don't have to come back to a place like this. Do you understand that?"

Joe looked up at them, tears streaming down his face. "You know what? No, I don't understand. I don't understand that, and I don't understand you. I don't know why you just don't leave me alone. *I told you I didn't want to see you.* I said *I didn't want you to come and see me in this place. Why is that so hard for you to understand?!*"

Joseph quickly stood up, pushing the chair back with his legs. "You guys need to leave before I lose it. Please just go."

He jammed his finger into the Assistance button, pressing it over and over again.

"Bud, if that is what you want, we will go home," Strapp said.

The guard appeared in the window and unlocked the door. He opened it a few inches and asked, "Is there a problem here?"

"No problem," Joe answered through gritted teeth. "I want to leave."

"Are you sure?" the guard asked. "You just got started."

"Yes, I am *sure*." His voice raised a decibel. "Do you think I would have pressed your stupid button if I wasn't sure? I want to go back to my cell."

The officer raised his eyebrows. He stepped into the room and said, "Okay, bud, if you say so. Hands behind your back."

As the guard put the handcuffs on Joseph again, Strapp stood.

He pulled a folded envelope from his back pocket. "Sir, is it okay if I give this letter to Joseph?"

"Let me see it." The guard took the letter out of the unsealed envelope and quickly unfolded it. He skimmed the words on the page, and he folded it again and put it in the envelope. "Yep, no problem. Here you go, son,"

"I don't want it," Joe said, his eyes on the floor.

"Yes, you do, young man," the guard said in a deep southern drawl. "Let me tell you something. You should feel real lucky right about now, you have no idea how good you have it. Not only do you have visitors, but you have both your mom *and* dad. Most of these kids in here don't have anyone come see 'em, let alone their parents. You understand, son? You are fortunate."

Joseph was silent.

Julie said, "Joseph…I love you."

"Me too, buddy," Strapp added. "We love you very much."

"Whatever," Joe said. "Please let me leave now."

The guard shook his head. "I'm sorry, folks. Hold tight while I take Joseph out. You will be let out shortly."

The guard unlocked the door, and he gestured for Joe to leave first. Strapp and Julie watched him shuffle his shackled feet toward the exit and out the door.

When the guard locked the door one more time, Julie startled at the sound. Nothing had ever sounded so *final.*

CHAPTER 22

When Joseph arrived back in his cell, he lay on his bed, tired, confused, and angry. With a little curiosity, he peeled back the enveloped and pulled out the folded pieces of paper. He began to read handwritten words from his dad.

Dear Joseph,

I love you. If you understand nothing else in this letter, please know that. Please hold those words, even if you cannot feel them.

I loved you before I met you, and I will love you longer than you can imagine.

You remember your life before me, and I will forever remember the day you became mine. But long before I knew your name I loved you.

I wanted you then, and I want you now. For you are my son.

I know that you feel abandoned right now, and that must hurt. But I want you to know that you are not alone. This may not make any sense to you, but I am beginning to understand your pain. I want you to know how sorry I am for what has happened to you. This world can be a very cruel place. No one should have to go through what you have experienced. I wish I could change it, but I just can't.

Right now, you have not chosen to see me as your father. It hurts me, but this is your choice to make.

I will continue to love you with an everlasting love. There is no end to my love. There will never be a finish line, a time when I will stop loving you. I will never leave you. There is no distance too far for me to travel to get to you, and there is no river so wide to keep us apart. Regardless of how high the mountain may seem or how deep and dark a valley you find yourself in, I will be there. Every step of the way.

When you are ready to come home, there will be a place for you—in my home and in my heart. I am your Father, and you are my Son. Nothing can ever change that. I will be waiting for you.

I will do everything in my power to rescue you, but I can't save someone who doesn't want to be rescued. The decision is yours.

Joseph, your mother and I chose you, and I want you to know that I would do it all again. I'll choose you again and again, and I will never stop choosing you, fighting for you, and loving you.

On this day, and on every day, I love you.

Dad

Joe folded up the letter. He lay in his bed, staring at the ceiling.

• • •

The next time Julie and Strapp saw their son, they were in a courtroom. Joe had been granted a hearing before a judge where a team would present the facts and ask the judge to determine the next steps: should Joe be moved to a residential facility, or should he be sentenced to jail? His fate rested in the decision of this day.

There were child development experts, counselors, a prosecuting attorney, a defense attorney, a parole officer, Joan the social worker, Dex the therapist, and of course, Strapp and Julie. And there was Joe—in handcuffs.

The judge listened as the team presented the long list of Joe's history, criminal behavior, and failed interventions. Strapp listened as well, and he couldn't deny the truth. The facts were compelling. Anyone might rightfully choose to give up on this young man.

"Does anyone else have any information to present?" the judge asked.

Strapp raised his hand. "Your Honor, if I may, I have something that I would like to say."

"Yes, Mr. Strapson. I'd like to hear your perspective before I make my decision."

Strapp stood before the judge, and he made one more plea for his son.

"Your Honor, I do not envy your position. Your decision is a difficult one. The history is compelling, the future does not feel promising, and I cannot disagree with the facts presented. Many interventions have failed, and I can understand why it would seem wise to put this young man behind bars."

Strapp paused. He looked at Joe, and the room watched as the father and son held each other's gaze.

And then Strapp turned to the judge and continued. "Your Honor, my son needs help. He needs therapy, not punishment. He has a lot of wounds, some that he has brought on himself, but most were given to him by this world. I firmly believe that if he continues to get the therapy he needs, he will have the best opportunity to become a productive member of this society."

"Your Honor," he continued, "my son is a good boy. He may be on the verge of adulthood by law, but he is really a little boy that is stuck in this teenage body. It would be a mistake to isolate him from society because I truly believe that community and family are the very things he needs to heal."

Strapp swallowed. He drew his hands together, and he said, "As his father, I stand before you now, humbly asking you to grant him restitution in a residential facility where he may get help, therapy, and assistance. He is a smart young man with a giant heart, and he has been failed by the actions of many people as well as the judgments of many systems. I'm asking you to give him another chance before committing him to jail."

"Anything further?"

"No, Your Honor. That is all I need to say."

"Thank you, Mr. Strapson. You may be seated."

Strapp returned to his seat next to his wife, as the judge said, "Joseph, you and your counsel will please rise."

Joe stood next to his attorney, and he waited to receive the judge's decision.

"Joseph Strapson, your father's plea has spared you today, young man. It is my ruling that you transition to a residential facility, where you will receive therapy, assistance, and interventions. Joseph, it is important on this day that you understand the components of mercy and grace."

"Yes, Your Honor," Joe said, not yet understanding the difference between the two words.

"Mercy is when you don't get the punishment you deserve, and grace is when you get a second chance. Today, you have been handed a double portion of each. I suggest you proceed wisely."

The judge looked up to scan the room. "Does anyone else have anything they would like to say?"

Joseph blurted out, "I do, your Honor."

"Son, I would recommend that you speak to your attorney before you say anything further."

Joseph's attorney quickly covered the microphone on the desk. Her eyes said everything that anyone would need to hear.

She turned to Joseph. "Listen very carefully to me right now, Joe."

"I just want to say…" he began.

"Joe—" she interrupted. "Look at me. Here is what you are going to say." She guided him to simply say "thank you," and then she held her breath, waiting to see if he would follow her counsel.

Joseph quickly squared his shoulders to face the Judge. "Your Honor, I just wanted to say thank you. I have been on the run for years now, and I am coming to realize that it is not what I want."

His voice began to crack, and tears formed in his eyes. "When I was on the streets, I was alone and afraid. I missed my family. I missed my team. I know that I will never be perfect, but I want to do the right thing. I am going to do my best, I really am."

Joseph awkwardly sat down. His attorney let out an audible sigh of relief.

The judge smiled and pounded his gavel, the punctuation of his verdict. "Court adjourned."

A security officer took the handcuffs off Joe, and he did not return to his jail cell. Strapp and Julie followed the county vehicle that transported their son to residential treatment facility—their place of hope.

CHAPTER 23

Hank furrowed his brow as he looked at Strapp's face. They were sitting at the same table where they had met for the first time. Strapp's face had new lines from worry, and his eyes were heavy with weariness. This father had loved so hard it had broken him.

Strapp took a sip of his coffee, and then he said, "Joe ran away from the residential facility, Hank. He's been missing for days. We have no idea where he is."

"Oh, no," Hank said, with deep earnestness.

"I've got to be honest, Hank, I've reached the point now where I'm out of energy. I'm out of answers. I'm out of emotion."

Hank said, "You sound like you are out of fuel."

"I am, Hank. And it's a tough spot to be in. I feel like I'm looking at God and asking what I'm supposed to do next."

"What do you hear him saying?"

"Well, part of me hears something like, *Now you know how much I love you.* But secondly, I'm learning that as a father, sometimes we must continue to pursue, even when we don't feel like it. I hear God telling me, just keep pursuing him."

"What does that pursuit look like right now?"

"Well, he's out of jail and in a residential facility again, but we'll see how long that lasts. I keep saying what needs to be said. I keep speaking truth to my son: I'm always here, I forgive you, and I love you. I'm never going to leave you, and I will help you in any way that I can. But I can't save him if he doesn't want to be saved."

"And how does that feel to you?"

"Helpless. And hopeless."

Hank nodded. "That's valid, Strapp."

"I mean, I'm learning a lot about the heart of God. Unlike me, God has the power to snap his fingers and fix everything. He has the ability to override free will if he wants to. He can even circumvent the consequences of this world if he chooses to. Sometimes he interjects himself in those ways, but in my experience, most of the time he doesn't."

"How hard must it be for God to have his children continually reject him?" Hank asked.

"Especially because he could fix it. I'd fix it right now if I could. But I'm not God. I don't have that ability to fix everything, and I also don't have an endless supply of love."

"The unconditional kind."

Strapp laughed and shook his head. "Yeah. Unconditional love. It sounds good—until it's tested. I don't have it in me."

"None of us truly do, not without the help of our heavenly Father. It sounds like you're at the end of your rope."

"I'm at the end of everything, Hank."

"That's when we can rely on God to be your strength and your love, Strapp. This is where he shines."

"Well, that's easier said than done, Hank. I'm not in the mood for that cliché."

Hank raised his eyebrows.

"Sorry, I know I'm not supposed to say that. I know, 'his strength is perfect when our strength is gone,' all of that. I know, okay? I know. But answers like that don't fix anything right now."

"Are people giving you lots of answers like that?"

"They mean well, I guess, but they say things like, 'I had a daughter who went off the rails,' or 'I was like him when I was his age, and I turned it around.'"

"What do you say to them?"

"I just nod because it is what it is. That's their experience, but so far it isn't mine. And stories like that don't do me any good."

"What do you want to say to them?"

Strapp laughed. "I want to say, 'I am not buying what you're selling right now.'"

Hank nodded. "That makes sense to me, Strapp."

"Sorry. It's a little raw."

"I'm okay with raw."

Strapp said, "Honestly, half of me is torn up, sad, worried, all of those things; all the emotions you would imagine. But the other half of me is extremely numb. When I'm talking about him—this, us—sometimes I feel like I'm talking about some other kid. Some other family I read about on the news."

"Like it's not even happening to you?"

"Yes. Like it's all happening to somebody else, and I'm just watching. I'm certainly not feeling."

"Is that a good thing?"

"It doesn't feel like a good thing. Who wants to be this detached from their own life? I don't like that feeling."

"Strapp, that sounds to me like a very natural coping mechanism. When you're dealing with any kind of pain, when the hurt goes deep enough, your body just stops feeling."

"That makes sense, no question."

"It shows how painful this is for you, Strapp."

Strapp's shoulders sank. "It seems like I should be crying about this right now, but I'm not. I mean, you get rejected so many times and eventually you stop putting yourself out there anymore. So, I guess if I seem pretty melancholy about this, it's because I am."

"Tired?"

"Tired. Yes. And frustrated. And unsure." He paused, and then he said, "Hank, in some ways—and I don't like this, even as I say it, but it's true, so I'm going to say it—in some ways, I feel like I'm losing hope."

"Strapp, let me ask you: do you have the freedom to feel how you feel?"

Strapp rubbed his chin. "I think so. I mean, a part of me must be okay with it, or I wouldn't be sitting here telling you all of this."

"That's true."

"However, there's a part of me that feels like none of these emotions are very *holy*. I don't exactly feel like a good parent."

"Do you think you're the first parent in the world to feel this way?" Hank asked.

"I know I'm not alone in these emotions."

"Yep. Absolutely. A lot of parents feel this way, especially when they're on a path like this one. And I guess if I can encourage you at all, I would say that there's much to grieve here. When you're dealing with the emotions and processes of grief, the feelings alone are enough to bury you. Simply feeling it is hard enough and telling yourself you shouldn't feel that way only makes it harder."

"That's true, man. That's so true."

"There's grace for you to walk in right now. Let yourself feel how you feel."

Strapp said, "I think it's okay to feel it, but I think it's also okay to just go through the motions. That's what I'm doing right now. I'm just trying to be obedient, even when I don't feel like it. Faithful, even though I don't feel like it."

"Strapp, that's what I meant when I said you could lean on the strength of God right now. You can keep going through the motions, keep doing the next right thing, even though you don't feel like it."

Strapp smiled. "Well, then that should be the cliché, not the empty words that don't make sense."

"That's fair, pal. Very fair."

"Hank, I'm learning that there are no guarantees in this; there are no promises I can cling to with Joe. There's no fill-in-the-blank, like if I do this, he'll do that. So, I just keep doing what seems to be the next right thing."

"And what does that show you?"

"I'm learning as I go."

"Say more about that."

"Well, I'm learning about me, I'm learning about God, and I'm learning about the things that are changing in me—even if they never change in my son."

"That's it, my friend. Spot on. Those are the disciplines of the faith, and that's why they're called disciplines: because they're hard, and sometimes we don't want to do it. But we remain disciplined, even when our emotions don't match what we must do next—whether that means praying, worshipping, reading, leading—whatever you're called to do. When you do it even though you may not want to, that's discipline. You know?"

"So, you're telling me that's okay?" Strapp asked.

"Yes, sir."

"And God's okay with it?" Strapp asked.

"Yes, Strapp. God's okay with it."

"Well, good. Because that's all I have to give him right now."

Just then, Strapp's phone buzzed with a text. Hank watched as Strapp looked at the screen, read the text, and met Hank's gaze.

"It's from Joe's phone."

"What does it say?"

"It's a notification. It says, 'Joe Strapson has shared his location with you.'"

"What does that mean?"

Strapp paused, his fingers clicking out a reply to his son.

"He says he's in a friend's car, and they're on their way to a motel. He says he's ready to talk."

Hank waited, watching Strapp.

Strapp put his phone down.

"Hank, I need to go find him."

"Then let's go," Hank said, grabbing his keys.

CHAPTER 24

Hank and Strapp tore down the highway in Hank's truck, racing to get to Joe. After so many days of not knowing where Joe was, Strapp could now track the GPS of Joe's moving locations. They were gaining on him, it seemed, following his blue dot on the map. Strapp texted Joe as Hank drove, but Joe sent no replies. Their only clues were the blue dots on the map. But as they got closer, Joe's dot moved further away.

Strapp had called Julie to tell her what he had learned, and she had agreed with him—he needed to go, but they also needed to alert the police about his contact with them. She called the authorities, and Strapp stayed in contact with her as they drove.

Then Joe's dot stopped moving on the map. Joe seemed to have stopped somewhere. Strapp's heart pricked with hope, and then he got a text from Joe.

It said, *I'm ready for you, Dad. I'm ready.*

Strapp replied, *I'm ready to help you, son. I'm on my way.*

He read the next message aloud to Hank. "It says, 'Village Inn Motel, Room 126.'"

"I know right where that is," Hank said. "We are ten minutes away."

For the next ten minutes, the dot never moved. There were no more texts from Joe.

• • •

Hank drove into the parking lot just as the police arrived. He pulled the truck up to room 126, and Strapp opened the door while the car was still moving.

Strapp pounded on the door. "Joe! Joseph! It's me. It's your dad. Joe!"

He pounded, pausing only to put his ear to the door to listen. There was no answer.

"Joe, the police are here, son. We want to help you."

No answer.

An officer came alongside him, pounding on the door. "Joseph Strapson? It's the Police. Open up."

No answer.

Strapp called out to his son again. "I'm here, Joe. We want to help you."

No answer. The officer burst through the door. They entered the room. Nobody was there. The room was empty.

Strapp's eyes looked at the things on the bed, each one a symbol of Joe breaking away. Joe's phone. The leather braided bracelet from Caroline. And a note scrawled on hotel stationery.

He picked up the note, and he read his son's words.

Stop following me.

I have told you so many times that I just want my own freedom.

I have tried to push you away and I just can't seem to shake you.

I don't know why you can't just see that this is who I am. I am never going to change.

I am tired of disappointing you and hurting this family, over and over again.

Leave me alone.

~ Joe

• • •

Hank waited in his truck as he watched the police officers overtake the room. He watched as Strapp went inside, and he held his breath as they all came back out—all without Joe.

Hank got out of his truck as he saw Strapp walk slowly out of the room, holding a slip of paper in his hand.

"Strapp?" Hank called to him, walking toward him.

Strapp took a few steps toward Hank, then his steps became a stagger, then a stumble. Strapp fell into Hank's arms, and he wept. This tall, bold man of such masculine strength—he cried hard. He wept years' worth of tears, over every unanswered question, and every dream that had broken in his hands.

He cried for his father. And he cried for his son.

Hank held him. He let him cry without shame, as only one man can do for another.

After Strapp caught his breath he stood on his own again. "I got bucked off the horse."

Hank thought of the horse barn, Shakespeare, and the cowboy falling off the wild stallion. He knew just what he meant. "He knocked you to the ground."

Hank waited. He watched Strapp, as he read the note again, his son's words. Then he saw him set his jaw. "What do you want to do?"

Strapp clenched his fist. "He. Is. My. Son."

His passion grew, louder and fiercer, with each word. And then he said, "With God as my witness, I will never give up. Never!"

"Mr. Strapson?" The police officer called out to him from across the parking lot. He had a radio in his hand, and Strapp could hear the muffled dialogue of officers talking back and forth. "We just got another lead from a detective. They may know where he is headed."

Strapp looked to Hank, and he pointed down the highway. With fire in his eyes, he said, "In the truck, Hank. Let's go get my son."

Hank grabs Strapp's arm, "Hold on a second."

"What do you mean, 'Hold on a second'?" He pulled his elbow out of Hank's grip. "We have to go! The police have a lead on him and we need to go find him."

"Strapp." Hank's voice was firm. He took Strapp's elbow again. "What is your plan?"

"My plan, Hank, is to find my son."

"And then what?"

Strapp thought for a moment. "Well, I guess we will load him up and take him home."

"You've taken him home before. What if he isn't willing?"

"Well, I guess we will cross that bridge when we get there. Let's go!"

"Son, before we do that, there is something I want to share with you that can dramatically change your life if you are willing to listen. Of all the things that I have shared with you over the last several years, this may be the most..."

"I know, I know." Strapp interrupts Hank. "But can't you wait to share this with me later? My son is on the run and time is slipping away. If we don't go now, we may never find him!"

"Strapp, look at me. Give me your eyes and listen to what I am about to tell you." Hank waited for him to lift his gaze and meet his eyes.

"There is a difference between chasing your son and pursuing him. When you chase someone, it is a relentless, all-out attempt to catch them. It is exhausting, frustrating, and unpredictable and there are no guarantees. I want you to consider something. At the end of the day, if we do catch up with Joseph and "trap him", and bring him home, what have we really accomplished?"

The look in Hank's eyes communicated that he wasn't looking for an answer.

"You can't hold him captive in a place he doesn't choose to be. That's not love."

Strapp is silent, his eyes filled with tears. "He is my son."

"Then pursue him as your son. Don't chase him like your prisoner."

"I... I don't know how."

"The answer is simple, but it is easier said than done. Let me explain it to you this way. You know the parable in the Bible when the shepherd leaves the 99 in order to go after the one that is lost?"

Strapp nods.

"Think about this for a minute. It doesn't say that he runs after the sheep. It doesn't say that he takes a net so when he gets close he can snag it and drag it home. Instead, he moves forward with a purpose. He is watching and waiting. He is waiting for the lone sheep to discover for itself that it is lost and it needs to be found. You see, there is a difference between a sheep that is running away from something and a sheep that is lost. The lost want to be found. Right now, Joseph doesn't want to be found."

"So what am I supposed to do? I can't just let him run? He might hurt himself. He might get caught up with the wrong people and then what? He is lost forever!" Tears begin to stream down Strapp's face. "I want to protect him. I just want my son to come home."

"I know you do. We all do. But he has to want it too and right now, he is running from the very thing that you are trying to give to him. If you pull him back now, he will be a captive slave, not a son."

As the words settled in the air, time stood still for Strapp. The sound of the police standing nearby and their radios chattering away became muted by the palpable presence of the Holy Spirit. His racing heartbeat began to settle and his quickened breathing slowed to a deep, relaxed pace. His gaze is narrowed and his ears suddenly became tuned to the voice of his Father.

"Now you know how I feel."

Strapp knew this voice. It was the voice that he heard years before, but this time He continued.

"Now make yourself easy to be found."

With those words, Strapp's perspective changed in an instant. Like the missing puzzle piece that brings the image all together, he could instantly see the connections between his many conversations with Hank. For the first time, he felt as though he had clarity on how to move forward.

Hank places his hand on Strapp's leg and gives him a slight nudge. "Strapp, are you with me? What's going on? Are you ok?"

In that instant, relief swept over Strapp. It was as if he had been swimming in deep waters and could finally come up for air.

"Hank I get it. I completely understand what you are saying."

"Talk to me, what did you hear?"

"He spoke to me again. God. He spoke to me again."

"What did he say to you?"

"Remember when I told you about that moment in the bathroom? Years ago, when I heard the voice that said, 'Now you know how I feel.'"

"Of course I do. Did you hear that again?"

"Yes, but this time he said something else. He followed that by saying, 'Now make yourself easy to be found.'"

Hank smiled and nodded. "What does that mean to you?"

"It means that I need to stop chasing him! I need to wait, I need to watch, and I need to pray. Pray that he will turn back."

"That is repentance, my friend."

Strapp takes a deep breath, "You know what's crazy? When we repent...when we turn back towards our pursuer...that is when He runs to us."

Hank's eyes narrow and a smile stretches across his face. "Yes, Strapp. That's what good fathers do."

"Sir." The policeman interrupts their conversation. "If you want to try and track him down, we really need to go. We can't wait any longer, we may lose him."

Hank looks at Strapp. "What do you want to do?"

"It's time to go home, so Joseph will know where to find me."

EPILOGUE

Probably not the ending you hoped for, was it? Me, neither.

Are you frustrated? Yeah, me, too.

I suspect you are probably upset—and maybe even a little heartbroken—that Joseph didn't wake up to his reality, turn from his rebellious ways, and change his heart to become the son that Strapp and Julie were dreaming of.

Stories aren't supposed to end like this. The good guy always wins, the prodigal son comes home, and the rainbow shines in the sky. It's how the good stories go, right?

Well, not in this case. Not in our story.

So far, there is no fairytale ending.

Let me explain.

First, let's talk about Joseph in the story. His character is patterned after my son, Peter.

Eleven years ago, my wife and I decided to adopt Peter. His story is his to tell, and it is even more complicated than the story of Joseph in this book. I can tell you this: I loved my son even before I met him, and I will love him for all his days. *He is my son.*

For many years now, I have felt the Lord telling me to write a book about this path, about my personal struggles as a father, and about the many challenges and lessons that the Lord taught us over that time. This story is inspired by our journey, and though some of the details in these pages are fiction, I wanted to tell a story like our own.

But when I considered writing the story, I kept coming back to one big problem: how would I write the final chapter? What if there isn't a happy ending?

For many years, I felt like I couldn't begin because I didn't know how to finish. We don't have a fairytale ending… we don't even have an encouraging one. I wanted the ending before I could start.

I wrestled and I waited. Seasons would come and go. Our hearts rose with hope, and then broke again with sadness. I kept thinking, "Surely, this year will be the turning point. Things will begin to improve, and he will embrace everything good that life has for him. Somewhere inside our son is a young man with dreams, aspirations, and plans to make a difference with his life. Maybe this will be the year when he will begin to use the many talents that we know he possesses."

So, I waited. I waited for answers, and for hope. I waited for the promise of a beautiful ending.

But then one day, I heard the voice of God. The Father said to me, "That ending is not the point of this book. It is about the journey."

And that's when I knew it was time to write this story. I had opened my hands to the possibility that this may be how it is, how it goes, how it ends for our family.

Hear me well: my dreams and hopes for Peter will never change, but the future of my family is not the point of this book. We may never have our happy ending, but I will never stop chasing after my son. *He is my son.*

Now let's talk about Hank.

If you have this kind of mentor in your life, someone with whom you can talk, reflect, listen, learn, drink coffee and grab a bratwurst, then count yourself blessed.

In real life, I didn't have a Hank—at least not how he is depicted in the book. For me, Hank has been the voice of the Holy Spirit. The Holy Spirit is the true teacher, the true mentor and friend. The Lord has taught me all these lessons over the years. His timing is always perfect, and his counsel is spot on, every time.

The Holy Spirit wants this friendship with you. He's waiting for you to call…just like Hank.

Now let's talk about you, my friend.

Perhaps you come from a very strong family unit, and you may have a healthy relationship with your mother and father. Or perhaps your home life may look quite the opposite. Regardless of your family history and your relationship with your parents, one thing is true: in the spiritual sense, you were born an orphan, just like me.

Just like Strapp chose Joseph, God chose you; long before you knew Him, long before you ever knew you needed Him. But here is the tragedy in the story: we weren't allowed to be in relationship with our heavenly father because of sin, and that left a huge hole in the heart of every person that has ever been born. That is the orphan's spirit.

The good news is that the story doesn't end there.

Unlike the story you just read, your story can have a perfect ending! God is willing to do everything it takes to get His kids back, and He paid the highest price for the sins of mankind. What was the price? The life of His own son. A monumental price to pay, wouldn't you agree?

God allowed Jesus to die on the cross for you and me. The sacred moment of the death of his son made our adoption possible. But the story doesn't end there. We get to choose.

Will we choose to be an *Orphan*, or to be a *Child of God*?

Even though Strapp chose to be a father to Joseph, Joe never chose to be Strapp's son.

The same decision has been placed before you in this moment.

Will you choose to be God's adopted child?

Your heavenly father is waiting for your answer.

Let me ask you these questions:

How do you see yourself in Joseph's story?

As Joseph rejected Strapp in this book, how do you reject your heavenly Father?

In what ways do you live and think as a son/daughter of God?

In what ways do you still think and live as an orphan?

If we are truly honest with ourselves, I believe we will begin to see that we aren't much different than young Joseph, who is always on the run.

My son isn't the only one with a battle raging inside him. Every single day, you and I have a war raging inside us as well. This is the battle between the orphan spirit and the spirit of sonship.

Some battle alcoholism. Some fight their addiction to drugs, gambling, or pornography, Some deal with pride, overeating, perfection, or the worship of money. Each of us has a unique "thorn in our side."

Each day, we have a choice: to walk as a son or daughter before a heavenly Father who has loved us since the beginning of time, or to reject His love, His name, His resources, and His protection—just as Joseph rejected Strapp. Each day, the Kingdom of Heaven hangs in the balance.

Which path will we choose?

If you have questions about this decision, or if you'd like someone to guide you through this choice, I invite you to go to jesuscares.com. There is a team of people waiting online, every hour of every day, and they are ready to chat with you. I pray that you will accept this invitation to become God's adopted son or daughter. Your life will never be the same.

God said, "I choose you."

Now, the choice is yours. Will you choose Him?

A LETTER TO MY SON

Peter,

Thank you for giving me permission to write this book. From the very beginning, I told you that I would not write a word of this if you weren't okay with it. You have shown a great deal of courage to allow me to share the intimate times we have had as a family, both the good and the bad. My prayer is that the lives of others will be changed because of your willingness to allow me to share what God has been teaching me through our relationship.

As you know, not everything that happened in this book is 100% accurate to your story; I made those changes for very specific reasons. I wanted to protect our family, but most of all, I wanted to protect your story. The details of your story are different than mine, but the storyline is very much the same. We all fall short of the glory of God and all of us are orphans in need of a Father. If you allow it, your story will one day become an incredible testimony for the world to hear.

As I write this, you are on the run. Not in the literal sense of running away from home, but you have presently chosen to run away from a relationship with me as your dad.

As long as I have breath, I will continue to pursue you. You may continue to run, or you may choose to come home. Either decision won't change the way I feel about you, I am proud to be your dad. Nothing will ever make me love you less, and nothing could ever make me love you more.

I will never leave you. I told you that the first day we got you, and I will keep that promise all the days of my life.

You are my son. That will never change.

I love you,
Dad

This picture was taken minutes after we first met Peter at the park. That first meeting was captured in Chapter 3 of this book.

ACKNOWLEDGEMENTS

This has been quite the journey. I have set many goals in my life, and I can honestly tell you that writing a book was never on the list—until about seven years ago. Even then, a dream of writing a book seemed unreachable. You know what I am talking about, it was a B.H.A.G. (Big Hairy Audacious Goal), much like my childhood dream to become a dolphin trainer at Sea World! Sounds cool, but hardly attainable. If I could quote a new friend of mine, Tricia Heyer, "A book is never written by just one person." This certainly couldn't be truer in my case.

First of all, I want to thank my new friend, Tricia. If not for her expertise, patience, and giftedness, this book would likely never have been written. This is my story, but when you see beauty in the words, fluidity in the story, and the gut-wrenching moments that pull you closer to the characters and prayerfully to God, that is Tricia. She was more than just a "ghostwriter." I would like to say that we co-created as we cried, laughed, and prayed our way through to the end.

I thank Matt Fontneau, Peter Heyer, Polly Lott, and Doyle Lott, who have read every word of this manuscript. They offered their expertise and perspectives to the story as parents, spouses, and therapists, and their contribution to the workshop carried us over the finish line.

I thank my beautiful wife Sherri (Julie) and my daughter Lindsey (Caroline). As the book began to unfold on paper, I quickly realized that although this is a work of fiction, this was not just my story—it is *our* story. In fact, I would say that 98% of everything you read in this book actually happened to our family, so I wanted to be sure that their "characters" were properly portrayed. Sherri and Lindsey collaborated during the final stages, and Lindsey designed and created the beautiful cover of the book. I am so thankful for your help and support through it all. You are two amazing women of God, and I thank you for helping me to become a better father, husband, and friend. I love you both very much.

I thank the men of the Remnant. Jon Sborov, Corey Bell, Ira Williams, David Fuess, Glenn Parker, Justin Lakin, Richard Lackey, Barry Wallis, Gary Carlson, Eric Fritzke, Mark Massey, Jeff Porter, Tommy Pasque, David Foley, Terry Shadwick, Randy Kenworthy, George Hanlon, Don Summers, JR Osborne, and Gene Osborne. You have all stood by me through this journey, and you have helped me to work through and process everything the Lord has been showing me. Thank you for helping me to refine my purpose and my message.

I thank my mom, who is my biggest fan. You have always cheered me on to bigger and better things. No one cares as much as you do. No one loves so unconditionally. I am especially proud for you to read this story, as no one has cared more.

I thank my dad, who is my biggest hero. Dad, you have been the rock for this family, and I want to thank you for your leadership. I see so much of our heavenly Father in you, and that has made my faith journey so much easier. You may have come to faith later in life, but you are finishing strong! If Hank's character is patterned after anyone, it is you. Thank you for always supporting me, as a mentor, friend, confidante, coach, and dad.

I thank the countless team of people that have done everything to support my family and my son Peter through this journey. To the teachers, principals, therapists, counselors, caseworkers, attorneys, guardian ad litem, policemen and women, probation officers, and numerous judges: thank you for the work you do and the ways you have served my family and me. You are the true heroes, and you are rarely recognized for your service.

Last, and certainly not least, I thank my son Peter (Joseph). Many years ago, I asked you if I could tell our story in a book, and you agreed. Thank you for trusting me and for having the courage to tell our story to the world. You are an amazing young man, and I hold great hope that you will find your way. Without you, this book would have never been written. My son, you and I share the same dream: that someone's life will be forever changed by the words in this book. But I hope your life is changed most of all. I love you, son.

Jeff Hutcheon travels throughout the nation, teaching and speaking groups about the principles of the Orphan Spirit and adoption. If you'd like to connect with Jeff on behalf of your family, small group, or church, contact Jeff at adoptedthebook@gmail.com.

Made in the USA
Coppell, TX
31 March 2021